"HELL OF A FIGHT, STRANGER."

Slocum buckled the belt on, glanced back once at Rhile, who was still wriggling on the ground, then headed for the door.

Behind him, Rhile had got up to his hands and knees. He stared hard at Slocum's back, killing in his gaze. He came to his feet with a sudden lurch, rushing to the gun holder before Slocum knew what had happened. Tolliver saw it, though.

"Slocum!" he shouted. "Watch out!"

Slocum pulled his Colt while spinning to his right and throwing himself to the side. Rhile's shot sounded first, the bullet going through the door of the building. Slocum's sounded like an echo, but it hit the mark. A black hole appeared in the middle of Rhile's chest . . .

DON'T MISS THESE
ALL-ACTION WESTERN SERIES
FROM THE BERKLEY PUBLISHING GROUP

THE GUNSMITH by J. R. Roberts
Clint Adams was a legend among lawmen, outlaws, and ladies. They called him . . . the Gunsmith.

LONGARM by Tabor Evans
The popular long-running series about U.S. Deputy Marshal Long—his life, his loves, his fight for justice.

SLOCUM by Jake Logan
Today's longest-running action Western. John Slocum rides a deadly trail of hot blood and cold steel.

BUSHWHACKERS by B. J. Lanagan
An all-new series by the creators of Longarm! The rousing adventures of the most brutal gang of cutthroats ever assembled—Quantrill's Raiders.

JAKE LOGAN

SLOCUM'S INHERITANCE

JOVE BOOKS, NEW YORK

SLOCUM'S INHERITANCE

A Jove Book / published by arrangement with
the author

PRINTING HISTORY
Jove edition / July 1997

The Putnam Berkley World Wide Web site address is
http://www.berkley.com

ISBN: 0-515-12103-7

A JOVE BOOK®
Jove Books are published by The Berkley Publishing Group,
200 Madison Avenue, New York, New York 10016.
JOVE and the "J" design are trademarks
belonging to Jove Publications, Inc.

PRINTED IN THE UNITED STATES OF AMERICA

10 9 8 7 6 5 4 3 2 1

SLOCUM'S INHERITANCE

1

Slocum scrunched down behind the boulder just as a slug hit it with a *zing* and ricocheted off to somewhere. It had been close, too close, and the rock, big enough for him to get down behind, was not big enough for any real comfort. Red Hat and at least two of his shooters were out there in front of Slocum, determined to fill him full of holes, and the guys on Slocum's side were somewhere behind, bringing up the rear, but not nearly fast enough to suit Slocum.

The bastards, he thought. If Red Hat and his boys kill me, they might get even, but by then I won't give a damn.

Another slug hit the boulder, and Slocum flinched. He longed for his Winchester, but it was in the saddle boot on his horse. When the Red Hats had started shooting, Slocum had taken a dive and rolled for the protection of the rocks. He hadn't taken time to think any farther ahead than that, so all he had was his Colt.

He wasn't sure just where the Red Hats were, how far out they might be, or how many of them there were. He only knew that he was caught in a trap. If he raised his head up to get a look, he might get it blown off. On the other hand, if he stayed hunkered down behind the rock, they might start moving in close and get right on top of him. It was a hell of a dilemma, and he didn't have any idea how he was going to get himself out of it alive.

1

Another slug hit the rock and yet another kicked up dirt just off to the right. By the sounds, one shot had come from a rifle, the other from a six-gun. The Red Hats were either close enough for six-gun shooting, or at least one of them was dumb enough to try long shots with one. He figured they must be pretty close.

He looked back behind, hoping to find a place to crawl to, but there was nowhere he could go without exposing himself to the shots from the Red Hats out there. He decided that he would have to do something. He thumbed back the hammer on his Colt, and was just about to raise up and look for a target, when he heard a barrage of shots, and they didn't seem to be coming his way.

He looked cautiously around the edge of the boulder, and out there in front he spotted Ready Joe and some of the boys from the Hang Dog spread. They must have heard the shots and circled around to slip up on the Red Hats. He stood straight up and grabbed the hat off his head with his left hand, waving it in the air.

"Get them, boys!" he shouted. "Hooray!"

He turned and trotted back to where his big 'paloose waited patiently for him, and he climbed into the saddle. Turning his mount, he rode toward the fight, but by the time he got there, it was over. He saw the bodies of Red Hat and the others lying there on the ground. Ready Joe and the others were still on their horses. Joe grinned as Slocum rode up beside him. He nodded toward the bloody corpses.

"How's that look to you?" he asked.

"Better them than me," Slocum said. "I was beginning to wonder if y'all were coming."

"Ah," said Ready Joe, "you just ain't got no patience." Then he raised his voice. "Let's gather up their horses and load up the carcasses. Old Clarence T. will be tickled pink to see this sight.''

Clarence T. was more than tickled. The range war between the Red Hat outfit and Clarence T.'s Hang Dog Ranch had been going on for some time. They were the two biggest ranches in the territory. Clarence T. had built his honestly. He was no angel. He had run over some folks along the way, but basically he was a hardworking and honest rancher. Red Hat, on the other hand, had been a big-time rustler who used his ranch as a front for his real business. Eventually Clarence T. had been forced to hire gun hands.

Clarence T. was tickled all right. He was so tickled that he paid out a big bonus, and he offered a permanent job to any of the gun hands who wanted to turn cowboy. A couple of them accepted the offer. Most pocketed the bonus and rode out in search of some fun. Slocum was one of the latter.

He wound up in a place called Frogtown. It was not too big, but it was lively and wide open. Built right on a major cattle trail, it was well prepared for the business a big cattle drive would bring, and in between it had more hotels and saloons than any little town needed. It was just what Slocum wanted.

When he first rode into town, he went all the way through, looking over the main street. Then he turned and headed back through, headed for the livery stable at the far end, where he had come in. He left his horse in the care of the stable man there, shouldered his blanket roll and Winchester, and walked back to a hotel he had spotted in the middle of town.

Called Frogtown's Best, it was certainly the biggest. Slocum went inside, paused, and looked around. He was standing in a big lobby, facing the counter across the way. To his left was an adjoining bar, and to his right a wide stairway led up to the rooms. Slocum walked across the room to the counter. The man on the other side looked up from his desk.

"Help you?" he asked.

"Where's the nearest place to eat?" Slocum asked.

"Right here," said the man, nodding toward the attached saloon.

"You got a room?"

"Got several," said the man, "till the next cow outfit comes through." He stood up and stepped to the counter, turning the hotel register around to face Slocum. "You want one?"

"I'll take one," Slocum said.

"Sign here."

While Slocum wrote his name, the man got a key and tossed it on the counter in front of Slocum.

"You can pay me now or pay me when you leave," he said. "Makes no difference."

Slocum dug down in his pocket for cash.

"I like to pay up front," he said. "That way I never get caught in a trap." The scene behind the boulder with Red Hat out front flashed through his mind. "Can I get a bath here?"

"I'll have it sent up."

Slocum picked up his gear and the key and started toward the stairs. Halfway there, he stopped and looked back over his shoulder.

"Say," he said. "Why's this place called Frogtown?"

The man behind the counter shrugged. "No one ever told me," he said.

Slocum went on up the stairs to find his room.

•   •   •

After a bath and in a clean set of clothes, Slocum felt like a new man. He bought himself a bottle of good bourbon and a couple of good cigars, ordered a steak dinner, and sat down at a table to wait. A tall, broad-shouldered man in a black three-piece suit walked into the room, paused, and headed straight for Slocum. He moved with a slight limp, but that fact made him seem no less formidable. Slocum could see the edge of a badge sticking out from under the man's coat. He stiffened, as he always did when confronted by a lawman. The man stepped up to the table where Slocum sat, and he looked down into Slocum's face.

Slocum stared back, trying hard to appear casual. It was a hard face he was looking into. Under the brim of his black hat, the man had cold steel eyes shaded by heavy brows that matched the thick mustache on his upper lip.

"You Slocum?" the lawman asked.

"That's right," Slocum said.

"I heard about that business with Red Hat."

"Well, I got no business here," Slocum said, "if that's what you're worried about. I'm just here to rest up a bit."

"Oh, hell," said the lawman. "Relax. You got me wrong. I'm not at all worried. You did a fine job on Red Hat. I'm just glad to have you here. I'm Tom Tolliver, town marshal. Welcome to Frogtown, Slocum."

"Well, by God," Slocum said, relaxing once again, "in that case, Mr. Tolliver, sit down and let me buy you a drink."

"Thank you kindly," Tolliver said. He pulled out a chair and sat across from Slocum, who was calling for another glass. When it was delivered, he poured it full and pushed it across the table to the marshal. He held his own glass up as for a toast.

"It's not often I get welcomed to town by the law," he said. Tolliver laughed and tossed down his drink. "Say," said Slocum, "how come they call this place Frogtown?"

"Damned if I know," said Tolliver. "The town was here before I came, and it already had that name. No one's ever told me why. Come to think of it, I never asked anyone, either."

Things were certainly looking swell. Slocum had money in his pocket, a nice room to sleep in, and he had already made friends with the local law. The whiskey and the cigars were good, even the steak dinner had been good. On top of all that, the prices were fair. They'd likely get jacked up when a trail herd came through, but in the meantime, he didn't know what else he could ask for from life. And just then, she walked through the door.

2

She spoke to the bartender but just passed him by, headed straight for the table at which Slocum was sitting with Tolliver. She was so beautiful, just looking at her nearly took Slocum's breath away. He realized that he was staring at her, wide-eyed and probably with a gaping mouth. He clamped his teeth together and forced himself to blink his eyes. She swept across the floor and came to a stop just across the table from him, standing right beside the marshal. The very air took on a new and sweeter smell.

"Hello, Tom," she said. "Are you going to introduce me to your friend?"

Her voice was like music, like a ringing of soft bells, and Slocum felt like an awkward young man again, a foolish feeling at his age, he thought, but he didn't care. He raked the hat off his head and stood up, almost overturning his chair in the process.

"This is Slocum," said Tolliver. "First name?"

"John," said Slocum.

"This is Lady Eve," Tolliver continued. "She's the owner of Frogtown's Best."

"It's a great pleasure, ma'am," Slocum said. He felt as if his tongue was incredibly thick. "Won't you join us?" he added, pulling out a chair. His heart was pounding in his chest as she moved to the chair he held.

"Thank you," she said, and she sat.

Slocum went back to his own chair and sat down again. He reached for the neck of his bottle, almost too eagerly, he thought.

"Can I get you a drink?" he asked.

"No, thank you," she said, and she glanced back toward the bar, raising a hand in a lovely and graceful gesture. "Ethan," she said.

"Yes, ma'am?" answered the bartender.

"Coffee."

Ethan went for the pot and soon brought to the table a steaming cup, which he placed there before Lady Eve. "Thank you," she said, and Ethan went back to his post behind the bar. A few customers had drifted in by this time, and a couple of ladies of the night had appeared at the bar. Slocum wasn't noticing. He wasn't interested in anything in the whole world other than the vision of loveliness sitting across the table from him.

"I haven't seen you around before, Mr. Slocum," she said. "Are you just arrived in town?"

"Yes, ma'am," he said.

"Are you two old friends?"

"About three drinks old," said Tolliver.

"We just met," Slocum said.

"Oh?"

"I knew his reputation," the marshal said. "He just helped clean out Red Hat and his gang, and so I wanted to meet him. You know," he went on, looking at Slocum, "I had a little run-in with Red Hat a few years ago myself. I'm still carrying a piece of lead around from it."

Slocum thought about the limp he had noticed earlier.

"Yes," said Lady Eve. "Well. We're glad to have you in Frogtown, Mr. Slocum. Are you planning to stay, or are you just passing through?"

"I haven't really thought that far ahead," Slocum said. "I just feel like having myself a nice long rest, and this looked like a good place to try to get it." He poured himself another drink and shoved the bottle toward Tolliver, who accepted it and refilled his own glass.

"I hope you find it so," said Lady Eve. "When the trail drives come through, it can get loud."

"That kind of noise doesn't bother me," Slocum said.

"Where are you staying, Mr. Slocum?"

"I got myself a room right here," he said.

"Wonderful," she said. "In that case, it's on the house for as long as you care to stay. And so are the meals and the drinks. No limit."

Slocum almost choked on his whiskey. He looked up at Lady Eve, disbelieving. "Why would you want to do that?" he asked.

"Out of gratitude," she said. "Because of what you did for Tom."

"I didn't do anything for him," said Slocum, "except buy him a few drinks. I never even saw him before just a little while ago."

"You may not have realized it at the time," she said, "but when you eliminated Red Hat, you did Tom a great favor. And me."

"I got paid for that job, ma'am," Slocum said, "and I can pay my way."

It suddenly occurred to Slocum that he was lusting after a woman who was already spoken for, and the man with the claim staked was sitting just across the table, looking at him and wearing a badge.

"I'm sure you can," she said, "but I insist. I'll make sure all the staff knows."

Slocum ducked his head. He guessed that he was licked on this deal. He decided that he'd give it up anyhow. He wasn't about to take on the town marshal. That just didn't seem the way to take a rest.

"Well, all right, ma'am," he said. "I'm sure not going to argue about it with you. I guess the marshal here must mean a lot to you."

"Well, yes," she said. "Of course." Tolliver nudged her in the side and gave her a look, then chuckled. "Oh," she said. "Oh. Of course. You didn't know. How would you? He's my brother."

Slocum looked at Lady Eve and pointed at Tolliver. "You," he said. "Your brother."

Tolliver laughed. "She's my sister, Slocum," he said. "And, yes, that means I'm her brother."

Slocum shoved a hand through his hair and leaned back in his chair. "Well, I'll be damned," he said. Then he laughed a little. "You know what I thought? I thought—"

Lady Eve chuckled, and the sound was like the tinkling of tiny bells to Slocum's ears. "Yes," she said, "I think we know what you thought."

"Well," said Slocum, reaching for his bottle, "I feel about three-quarters fool."

Just then a dapper-looking man in his mid-thirties walked into the room. He paused at the bar, and when Ethan spoke to him, he shook his head. He was wearing a gray suit with a bowler hat, and he sported a trim little mustache under his nose. He spotted Slocum and headed straight for him. Stepping up to the table, he pulled off his bowler to reveal a shiny bald head. He glanced at Lady Eve with a slight bow.

"Excuse me," he said, then turning toward Slocum added, "Mr. John Slocum?"

Slocum wrinkled his brow. "Yeah," he said, "that's me."

"My name is Blenstool. I'm a private detective."

"A what?" Slocum asked.

"A private detective," said Blenstool. "You know, like Mr. Sherlock Holmes."

"Who?" Slocum asked.

"You mean like a Pinkerton man?" Tolliver asked.

"Yes," said Blenstool. "May I sit down?"

"I'm not wanted for anything," said Slocum. "You're on the wrong trail."

"May I?"

"Yeah," said Slocum. "Go ahead."

Blenstool pulled out a chair and sat next to Slocum. He placed his bowler carefully on the table in front of him.

"Mr. Slocum," he said, "private detectives are hired for reasons other than tracking down fugitives. I was hired by a Mr. Rundel Lewes, an attorney in St. Louis, to locate you."

Blenstool had everyone's full attention by this time. Lady Eve and her brother the marshal were paying as close attention to the detective as was Slocum.

"How the hell did you find me here in Frogtown?" Slocum asked. "No one knew I was coming here. Hell, I didn't even know it till I got here."

"It wasn't easy, Mr. Slocum, believe me," said Blenstool.

"Well, what does this—what'd you call him?"

"Mr. Lewes."

"What does this lawyer want with me?"

"Mr. Slocum," said Blenstool, "do you recall an uncle on your maternal side?"

"You mean, uh, my mother's brother?" Slocum said. "Well, yeah, Uncle Ferdie. Hell, I haven't thought about him in years. We weren't very close, me and him. I don't know anything about him, really. What's he got to do with this?"

"He's dead, Mr. Slocum."

"Dead?"

"Yes."

"Well, like I said, we weren't close. I don't reckon it was worth your while to come all the way out here just to tell me that."

"Mr. Slocum," said Blenstool, "your uncle Ferdinand left a will, and you are named as one of the heirs. Mr. Lewes hired me to find you and bring you back to St. Louis for the reading of the will."

"What?"

"I said—"

Slocum waved a hand to silence Blenstool. "I know what you said. I just—well, I hate to send you back empty-handed, mister, but I'm not interested. I don't know what old Ferdie left behind, but I don't want any part of it. I never did anything for him, and he never did anything for me, and I think it's best just to leave it like that. I make my own way in this world. Sorry, Pard, but a trip to St. Looey just don't fit my plans."

"Mr. Slocum," said Blenstool, "I hope you'll reconsider. My instructions are to bring you back to St. Louis with me."

"That's too bad," said Slocum. "Here, have a drink for your trouble. I'll sign a little note for you to prove that you found me, if that'll help, but I'm staying right here for a while."

Lady Eve called for another glass, and Slocum poured Blenstool a drink and shoved it over beside the bowler. The detective studied the glass there before him.

"Mr. Slocum," he said, "I don't think you quite understand. Your uncle Ferdinand was quite explicit in the terms of his will. All of the living heirs must be present for the reading."

"Hell, tell them I'm dead then," said Slocum. "We can get the marshal here to sign that note. That ought to satisfy them."

"I can't do that, Mr. Slocum," said Blenstool. "That would be dishonest."

Slocum heaved a long and heavy sigh. "Look," he said, "I'm sorry about your problem, but it is your problem, not mine. You figure out how to deal with it. Would you all excuse me for just a minute?"

"Of course," said Lady Eve.

Slocum shoved back his chair, stood up, and walked over to the bar to stand beside one of the ladies there. Lady Eve's gaze followed him, curious. She saw Slocum pull some cash out of his pocket and hand it to the lady known as Lou. Then Slocum and Lou looked back toward the table. Slocum patted Lou on the ass, then walked back to his chair to sit down again and pour himself another drink.

"Mr. Slocum," Blenstool started, but Slocum stopped him.

"Leave it alone, Pinkerton man," he said.

"I don't work for the Pinkerton Agency," said Blenstool, a little miffed. "I am a private detective, but the Pinkertons are not the only detective agency in the country. Mr. Slocum—"

Just then Lou stepped up close behind Blenstool and put her hands on his shoulders. He stiffened at the surprise and turned his head just in time to see her lower her face to kiss the top of his head. His face and the top of his head blushed.

"What—"

"Hi," said Lou. She leaned around so she could look him right in the face, and she stroked the side of his head with her hand. "God, you are cute. You're out here from St. Louis all by yourself?"

"Really, Miss—"

"Lou," she said. "Call me Lou."

She wriggled around until she could squeeze in between Blenstool and the table and sit down on his lap. She stroked his face and his bald head with both her hands.

"You're some kind of detective?" she said. "I think that's exciting."

She gave a little shiver, then, holding his head between both her hands, she kissed him full on the lips. Blenstool started to resist, meant to protest, but Lou was a luscious young lady, and she was beginning to cause a stirring in his loins.

"We could be a lot more comfortable upstairs," Lou whispered in his ear. Blenstool felt his rod stiffen and push at his trousers. So did Lou. She reached down to give it a squeeze. "Don't worry," she whispered. "It's all taken care of already."

Blenstool shot Slocum a glance. Then he at last put an arm around Lou.

"Yes," he said. "Upstairs will be much better."

Lou stood up, taking the detective by his hand, and pulled him to his feet. Blenstool picked up his bowler and looked at Slocum.

"Excuse me, Mr. Slocum," he said, "I, uh—"

"Go on," said Slocum. "Hell, I'll still be here in the morning."

As Tom Tolliver laughed, excused himself, and left the room, Lou led Blenstool to the stairway in the next room and then up to a room at the far end of the hall. She opened the door and walked in, and Blenstool followed. He shut the door, and Lou reached over to hook the latch. Then, looking at him suggestively over her shoulder, she moved toward the bed while unfastening her bodice.

Down in the saloon, Slocum was wishing that he and

Lady Eve had been the pair going up the stairs together. He was trying to work out in his mind the best approach to Her Ladyship, when a hulking drunk turned away from the bar and weaved his way over to the table to stop beside her.

"Come on and have a drink with me, Lady Eve," he said.

"No, thank you, Rhile," she said.

"Come on," said Rhile. "You've been here long enough. Ain't you supposed to move around a little? Make yourself available to different customers?"

"I'm not one of the girls," said Lady Eve. "I'm the boss, and I make myself available where and when I want. Now, run along, Rhile."

"You never will drink with me, and I'm tired of getting snubbed like that." He grabbed Lady Eve by the arm, starting to pull her to her feet. "Who is this bastard anyhow?" he said. "He ain't no better than me. Come on."

Slocum stood quickly, knocking his chair over backward. His Colt was in his hand and cocked. Rhile stopped still and loosed his grip on Lady Eve's arm.

"I think I'm better than you," said Slocum. "Let's go outside and find out."

"Fight!" someone yelled.

"Slocum," Lady Eve started to protest.

"It's all right, ma'am," said Slocum. "This fellow needs to be taught a lesson in manners." He gestured toward the door with the barrel of his Colt. "Come on," he said.

Rhile puffed out his chest.

"You put down that gun," he said, "and I'll break every bone in your body."

"I'll put it down," said Slocum, "outside. And we'll see whose bones get broke."

The whole crowd followed Slocum and Rhile out into

the street. Slocum picked out a man in front of the crowd who didn't appear to be too drunk.

"Will you hold our guns?" he asked.

"Be proud to," the man answered.

"Shuck yours," Slocum said to Rhile.

Growling threats, Rhile unbuckled his gun belt and handed it to the man. Slocum holstered his Colt then and did the same. Then the two squared off in the middle of the street. The crowd started roaring encouragement. About then, Tolliver appeared. He stopped beside his sister there on the sidewalk.

"What's all this?" he asked.

"Rhile was bothering me," she said, "so Slocum's defending my honor. I tried to stop him."

Tolliver stepped out into the street between the two would-be combatants.

"Hold on," he said.

"You stay out of this," snarled Rhile.

"Is there any law against a fistfight in this town?" Slocum asked.

"Well, no," said Tolliver. "I guess not, but there's something you ought to know."

"Never mind about that," said Slocum. "This fight has got to take place."

3

The crowd, having followed Slocum and Rhile out into the street, soon had them surrounded. They pushed and shoved, seeking better advantage, and shouted encouragement to help get the fight started the sooner. Some among them placed quick bets on one fighter or the other. Slocum wasn't at all surprised about the crowd's behavior. He figured that any real entertainment in Frogtown was at the most infrequent.

Rhile spit on his hands, doubled his fists, and held them up in a ready position. Slocum responded by putting up his own guard. "Come on, you piece of shit," he said.

Rhile roared and rushed at Slocum, taking a wild swing with his right. Slocum sidestepped it easily and tapped Rhile on the side of the head as he passed by. Rhile ran right into the crowd, where several hands stopped his forward progress, turned him around, and pushed him back toward Slocum. He stood glaring at Slocum and rubbed the sting on the side of his head.

"One of them fancy fighters, are you?" he said.

"Not so fancy," Slocum said. "You're just clumsy."

Rhile moved toward Slocum again, this time more slowly. He bobbed his head, and Slocum missed a jab. Then Rhile swung wide, a right and then a left. His punches missed the mark, but his arms wrapped around Slocum in

17

a bear hug. Slocum pounded Rhile's gut a few times, until Rhile hugged him too tightly and his arms were pinned.

Slocum tucked his chin and shoved the top of his head into Rhile's neck, driving Rhile's head up and back. Rhile groaned and squeezed harder as Slocum reached around Rhile's leg with his own, then shoved hard forward, driving Rhile over and onto his back. He landed hard with Slocum's full weight on top of him, and the force of the landing jarred the wind out of his lungs and loosened his grip at the same time. Slocum rolled to his left, then got quickly to his feet.

Not allowing Rhile time to recover his breath, Slocum grabbed his shirtfront and pulled him to a standing position. Then he drove a right followed by a left hard into Rhile's gut. Rhile hugged his belly, leaning forward. Slocum stepped back and swung a wide and hard right. His fist crashed into the side of Rhile's head, knocking him over sideways.

"By God," someone said, "he's out."

"No, he ain't out," said another, "but he ain't getting up neither."

Rhile groaned and squirmed in the dirt, but he made no attempt to stand up for more. Slocum stood over him for a moment, then said, "I think the fight's over folks." He looked over his shoulder for the man holding the guns, spotted him, and walked over there to retrieve his gunbelt.

"Hell of a fight, stranger," said the man, handing the rig back to Slocum. Slocum buckled the belt on, glanced back once at Rhile, who was still wriggling on the ground, then headed for the door back into Frogtown's Best.

Behind him, Rhile had got up to his hands and knees. He stared hard at Slocum's back, killing in his gaze. He came to his feet with a sudden lurch, rushing to the gun holder and jerking his own revolver out of its holster almost before the astonished man knew what had happened. Tolliver saw it, though.

"Slocum!" he shouted. "Watch out!"

Slocum pulled his Colt while spinning to his right and throwing himself to the side. Rhile's shot sounded first, the bullet going through the door into the building. Slocum's sounded like an echo, but it hit the mark. A black hole appeared in the middle of Rhile's chest. He stood for a moment with a stunned look on his face. The life went out of his fingers first, and the revolver slipped from his hand to fall into the street. He wobbled slightly, then dropped to his knees. Finally, the life gone from his body, he fell forward on his face.

Slocum holstered his Colt and walked on into the bar, going back to the table where his drink still waited for him. He picked up the glass and drained it in a gulp. Tolliver and Lady Eve came up to the table just then.

"I tried to warn you," said Tolliver, "but God damn it, you just wouldn't listen, would you?"

"Why?" Slocum asked. "What's wrong?"

"What's wrong? You killed Rhile Sut," said Tolliver. "That's what's wrong."

"The son of a bitch tried to backshoot me," Slocum said, somewhat indignant. "I'd call that self-defense, and there was a whole damn town out there for witnesses."

"I ain't disputing that, Slocum," said Tolliver. "Hell, Rhile's had it coming for a long time. And once he drew down on you, you had no choice but to kill him."

"Then what the hell are you getting at?" Slocum asked.

"Your choice was earlier," Tolliver said. "You shouldn't have let yourself get drawn into a fight with the bastard."

"I don't get it," Slocum said. "What the hell's your problem?"

"It's not my problem," Tolliver said. "It's yours. And it's Rhile's family. As soon as the Suts get the word, old Pop Sut's going to come in here looking for you, and he's going to have his family right behind him. All of them."

Slocum sat down and reached for his bottle. He poured himself another drink. Without bothering to look up at Tolliver, he said, "How many is all of them?"

Lady Eve took her former seat across the table from Slocum just then, and Tolliver looked down at her.

"How many would you say, Sis?"

"Six, at least," she said. "That's just Pop and Rhile's brothers. Then there's cousins. I'm not sure how many."

Slocum took a sip from his fresh drink, then held the glass in front of his face. He appeared to be studying it, but he was studying the fix he had gotten himself into. He had thought that Frogtown was going to be a nice place to take it easy in for a while. He had been looking forward to a long period of ease and comfort and maybe even a little fun. He had even imagined, after having met Lady Eve, that perhaps he would have some of that fun with her.

Now because of a stupid clod with no manners and an overblown sense of his own abilities, all that had gone up like a cloud of cigar smoke dissipating in the wind. Slocum was no coward, but neither was he a fool. He had no intention of waiting around Frogtown for at least a half dozen men, and maybe more, to ride in with the intention of killing him. He wouldn't even know who they were when they arrived. He'd be watching every stranger, waiting for one of them to take a shot at him. There would be no rest and no fun in that. None at all.

"God damn it," he said, and took another drink. He looked at Tolliver. "About how long would you say I've got around these parts before I start dodging bullets?" he asked.

Tolliver looked at Lady Eve. She had a worried expression her face.

"I saw Oliver ride out of town right after the shooting," she said.

"He's a friend of theirs," Tolliver explained. "I reckon they'll get the word before the night's over. They could come riding into town in the morning."

"Well, shit," said Slocum. Then, with a glance toward Lady Eve, he said, "Excuse me, ma'am. Well, it's been a short and sweet visit. I'd meant for it to be a longer one, but I believe in avoiding trouble whenever I can. Where do you reckon that young lady took the detective to a while ago?"

"I imagine the last room on your right at the end of the hall upstairs," Lady Eve said.

"Thank you, ma'am," said Slocum, and he got up and headed for the stairway.

Lady Eve and Tolliver gave each other questioning looks, and Tolliver shrugged.

Slocum climbed the stairs, walked down the hallway, and opened the door to the room without any hesitation. Lou's eyes opened wide in surprise, and her mouth opened as if to scream, but she didn't scream.

She was on the bed, sitting up, almost, leaning back against the headboard. Her legs were spread wide, her knees up, and Detective Blenstool was on his hands and knees, his bare ass up in the air, his face buried in Lou's crotch. Slocum slammed the door behind himself, and Blenstool jumped.

He turned around, sitting down on the bed with Lou's feet on each side of him, and wiped at his mouth with the back of his arm.

"Really, Mr. Slocum," he said. "You might have knocked."

"I don't have time to be polite," Slocum said. "Get your clothes on. We're leaving."

"Now?"

"Right now."

"What made you change your mind?"

"Never mind about that," Slocum said. "Just get dressed, and let's clear out."

"Well, at least wait for me out in the hall," said Blenstool.

"All right," said Slocum, "but don't mess around. I ain't waiting, and if you're not out here when I'm ready to go, you'll have a hell of a time finding me again."

Slocum stepped out into the hall and shut the door behind himself, leaving Blenstool alone in the room again with Lou. The little detective started to get up, but Lou grabbed him around the shoulders and pulled him down again between her legs. Then she wrapped her legs tightly around him. Blenstool started to melt. Then he reminded himself of his professional duty and the job at hand.

"Please," he said, "I have to go."

"Oh," said Lou, "let him wait. We were having so much fun."

"Yes, but—"

"Weren't you having fun?"

"Yes, indeed I was," said Blenstool, "and if it wasn't for duty calling, nothing would get me out of this room right now. But I have a job to do, and if I don't get out of here right now, I might not be able to get it done. Please let me go, lovely little lady."

He leaned forward and kissed her on the lips, and she in turn rubbed his shiny bald head with both her hands. Blenstool, with a mighty effort, pulled himself free and hurried into his clothes. At last he topped his bald head with the derby and made a courteous bow to the lady known as Lou.

She blew him a kiss, and he went out into the hall to join Slocum.

"Let's go," Slocum said.

"Have you determined how we're going to leave town at this hour?" Blenstool asked.

"Ride out," said Slocum.

"I'll have to hire a horse," the detective said. "I came by rail as far as Kellyville. From there to Frogtown I rode a stage."

"Then we'll get you a horse," Slocum said.

"Is the livery open for business?"

"I don't know," said Slocum, "but I know where there's a horse without a rider."

"You're not talking about stealing a horse, are you?" Blenstool asked with wide eyes.

"Not exactly," said Slocum. "Come on."

He led Blenstool back down into the bar, where Lady Eve and Tolliver still sat at the same table where Slocum had left them just before. Slocum looked at Lady Eve.

"Ma'am," he said, "I've decided to let this detective here take me to St. Louie with him after all. I surely do hate leaving—your town so soon."

"A wise decision, Slocum," said Tolliver.

"Can you point out Rhile Sut's horse to me?" Slocum asked the marshal.

"Sure. What for?"

"I don't reckon he'd mind any," said Slocum, "if we was to borrow it for a ride over to Kellyville."

Tolliver shrugged. "I guess not," he said. "Come on."

Soon Slocum was mounted on his big 'paloose, his blanket roll tied on behind the saddle. Blenstool was riding what had been Rhile Sut's mount, trying to hang on to a carpetbag. They rode out of town in silence, but a couple of miles down the road, Blenstool at last spoke up.

"Damn you, Slocum," he said. "You picked a damned inconvenient time to change your mind."

"You wanted me to go back with you," Slocum said.

"Yes, but you refused, and it was you who set that lady on me in the first place. You did that just to get rid of me. Didn't you?"

"I confess," said Slocum. "I did that."

"What changed your mind just at that time?"

"I had to kill a man back there," said Slocum.

"The gunshots I heard?" Blenstool asked.

"The first shot was his," Slocum said. "It missed."

"But you're not running from the law," said Blenstool. "We just said our good-byes to the town marshal."

"The man I killed was named Rhile Sut," said Slocum. "Tolliver told me that he comes from a big family, and they'll all be after me tomorrow."

"Oh, shit," the detective said. Then he added, "Excuse me, but shouldn't we be hurrying on?"

4

Blenstool was a competent enough horseman, but he was obviously uncomfortable, and Slocum knew that the little detective would be much more at home once they had climbed aboard the train at Kellyville. To his credit, though, Blenstool was not complaining, and they had ridden most of the night. The eastern sky just along the horizon was beginning to show signs of light as they topped a rise. Before them, the road wound down into a valley and up the other side.

"You recognize this place?" Slocum asked.

"When we ride up out of the valley on the other side," Blenstool said, "we'll be able to see Kellyville ahead of us. We're almost there."

"Good," said Slocum. The sooner he could put serious distance between himself and the Suts, the better he would feel. "What time's the train east out of Kellyville?"

"I believe," said Blenstool, "there's one leaving at ten in the morning. We should be there in plenty of time to catch it."

"That sounds just fine to me," Slocum said. He leaned back in the saddle as the big 'paloose started the descent into the valley. Blenstool failed to make the adjustment soon enough. He felt himself thrown forward, but he did manage to right himself before actually losing his seat. Neither man spoke again as they rode down into the valley and across. Ahead of them, the road up to the other side was lined with rugged boulders. Slocum was just about to kick his big stallion in the sides to urge him up the hill, when he saw a hat ease up from behind a boulder.

"Ambush!" he shouted. He threw himself to his left out of the saddle, dragging his Winchester along with him. When he hit the dirt he rolled, and then he scampered behind a rock. It was not big, but it was near. He had to crouch behind it for security. Only an instant behind him, Blenstool dropped his carpetbag, swung a leg over his mount, and ran for cover in a crouch. A rifle shot rang out from up above, and a slug spanged against a rock just behind Blenstool. The little man dropped behind a boulder not far from where Slocum huddled.

"Suts?" Blenstool asked.

"They sure move fast," Slocum said.

He peered around the edge of his protective rock, and another shot rang out. He ducked back quickly as the slug zinged against his shield. He popped up and took a quick shot, and he saw the bushwhacker drop out of sight—too soon. He hadn't been hit. He'd ducked in time.

"Damn it," he said. We could be here like this all day, he thought, or until someone runs out of ammunition. And if we're held up here for even half the morning, we'll miss the god damned train.

"Mr. Slocum," said Blenstool.

"What?"

"If anything should happen to me here, or anywhere else along the way, you'll find a letter in my pocket from your uncle's attorney, Mr. Rundel Lewes. It will tell you everything you need to know about where to go and who to see in St. Louis."

"Bullshit," said Slocum. "We'll get out of this."

He wasn't nearly as sure of that boast as he pretended to be.

"Nevertheless," said Blenstool, "I want you to know about the letter. Get ready with your rifle. I'm going to draw that man's fire."

"Don't be a fool, Blenstool," Slocum said.

"We don't have time for this waiting game," the detective said. He drew out of his coat pocket a British Webley Bulldog revolver and cocked it. He looked around and spotted another boulder not too far off that would afford protection. That was his goal. "Now, Slocum," he said, and he stood and ran for the other boulder, firing the Webley as he ran.

The man on the rise popped up and aimed for Blenstool, and Slocum fired. The man gave a jerk and dropped his rifle, which went clattering down the hillside. Blenstool was just about to dive behind the boulder when a second man appeared from above and fired a round. Blenstool yelled, dropped, and scampered for cover. Slocum cranked another shell into the chamber of his Winchester and fired again, but the second shooter had disappeared.

"Blenstool," he called.

"I'm all right," came the answer.

"Are you hit?"

"Not bad."

"Shit," Slocum hissed to himself. Blenstool's ruse had worked, but only so far. Slocum had got the man they were after, but they hadn't known there was another. And now Blenstool was hit. Slocum didn't know where or how badly, and he had no idea how much the little detective's wound would slow them. That, of course, was assuming that they could find a way of getting the second shooter. And were there more?

Ordinarily Slocum would have had the patience to wait

out a situation like this, but he did want to catch that ten o'clock train, and he didn't want to delay too long while Blenstool lay bleeding over there. Too much bleeding could make even a minor wound into something much more serious. He told himself that he was going to have to think of something real soon.

"Mr. Slocum," said Blenstool.

"What?"

"Get ready."

"Get ready, my ass," said Slocum. "You just sit tight, you little son of a bitch."

"Now, Mr. Slocum," said Blenstool, and he rose up from behind his rock, aimed his pocket pistol, and fired three rapid shots in the general direction of the ambusher. Sure enough, the man appeared again and leveled his rifle at Blenstool. Slocum aimed and fired quickly, and the man spun and fell out of sight behind the boulder on the side of the hill.

"Good shot, Mr. Slocum!" shouted Blenstool.

Then a third man came out from hiding in the large boulders, but he was mounted and riding hard for the top. Slocum started to fire at him, but decided against it. He lowered his rifle and watched the man disappear over the top. Then he trotted over to Blenstool's side.

"Where're you hit?" he asked.

Slocum saw the blood even as he heard Blenstool's answer.

"He nicked the back of my calf," said the detective. "Left leg."

Slocum bandaged the leg as best he could, caught up the horses, and helped Blenstool into the saddle.

"We'll see if we can find you a doc in Kellyville," he said. "That was a damn fool thing to do, you know." Actually, but secretly, he was admiring the little man's boldness. He had a whole new attitude toward Blenstool. The man had guts and integrity, and Slocum respected both of those qualities.

They had ridden about halfway up the hill on their way out of the valley when Slocum halted his mount. He swung down out of the saddle, pulled out his Colt revolver, and made his way cautiously toward the boulder behind which the first shooter had been secreted. Blenstool sat in his saddle, watching and waiting in silence. Soon Slocum made his way back to the road and remounted.

"Let's go," he said.

"Both dead?" Blenstool asked.

"Deader'n hell," Slocum said.

"Did you recognize either of them?"

"I never saw them before," Slocum said, "but one of them bore a hell of a resemblance to old Rhile Sut."

"One got away," Blenstool said. "We'll have to stay alert."

"You got that right," Slocum said.

In Kellyville they found a doctor and had Blenstool's wound properly dressed. They also reported to the sheriff, giving him the details of the ambush in the valley.

"Suts," said the sheriff. "They was in town early this morning. Seems they had a wire from old Pop Sut over by Frogtown last night."

"That's how they got ahead of us," Slocum said.

"These you ran into this morning," the sheriff said, "live over this way. They're cousins of that other bunch. But they're all real close. A real clannish bunch. I got a wire from Frogtown, too. From Marshal Tolliver. He told me what happened over there, and what was likely to happen over this way. You taking the train out of here this morning?"

"That's our intention," Slocum said.

"Best thing you can do," said the sheriff. "Short of killing the whole family."

From the sheriff's office the two unlikely companions stopped by the general store, where Blenstool selected himself a walking stick. Then they went to the depot to buy their tickets. Slocum insisted that his horse be taken along, too, and Blenstool paid for its transport out of his expense account. They still had an hour before departure time.

"How about some breakfast?" Blenstool asked.

"You bet," said Slocum.

They found a likely looking place just next door to the depot, went inside, and sat at an available table. Soon a stocky, middle-aged man in a greasy apron took their order. Slocum and Blenstool both kept looking all around themselves, studying the faces of all the men they could see. Everyone looked like a Sut or a Sut friend and ally. The greasy waiter brought them coffee, and as they slurped the hot, steaming liquid, they continued to watch the passersby on the street through the big front window of the place. They had two cups of coffee each before their meals were served to them. They ate hearty and had more coffee. They still had twenty minutes.

Then the train arrived, its shrill whistle splitting the air. They felt the building shake as it pulled up to the depot, spitting steam with a loud hissing noise and filling the air with smoke and cinders and all the smells of burning wood and oiled metal parts. When it had come to a full stop, passengers disembarked, baggage was unloaded, and more baggage was loaded. Slocum watched as his horse was led up a ramp into a boxcar. He and Blenstool sat in chairs on the board sidewalk in front of the depot, their backs against the wall, to wait for the time for boarding. Slocum noticed Blenstool feel the Webley in his coat pocket. In spite of himself, he gripped the handle of his Colt. He wondered where the third bushwhacker had gone.

He might have gone back to report the failure of his mission to the rest of the family, or he might be lurking about town waiting for another chance. He might be alone, or he might have others with him. Slocum knew that he had to be ready for anything. He figured that Blenstool knew that, too, and after the events in the valley that morning, he wasn't worried about the little detective. He knew that Blenstool would do his part.

"How much time?" he asked.

Blenstool pulled a watch out of his pocket and studied it. "Another fifteen minutes or so," he said. He tucked the watch away quickly, as if he didn't want even his left hand to be tied up for too long.

"Blenstool," he said, "this situation is just too damn nervous for my taste. If we don't get hauled out of this town pretty damn soon, I'm going to go hunting Suts."

"I understand the feeling, Mr. Slocum," said Blenstool. "Try to control it. We should be boarding real soon now."

Blenstool was right, for in another few minutes the conductor called, "All aboard." They climbed aboard the nearest passenger car and found themselves a seat at the far end, their backs against the wall. Still nervous, they studied the face of every male passenger who came into the car.

"Is this son of a bitch ever going to go?" Slocum asked.

Blenstool didn't bother answering. The question wasn't meant to be answered. But it wasn't a minute later when the whistle blew and the train lurched, starting on its way. Slocum sighed a heavy sigh, but it wasn't real relief, not yet. He had no idea who all had gotten aboard at the Kellyville depot, and he knew that if he, himself, had been after someone, really after someone, he wouldn't let a train ride out of town stop him.

"You're still expecting trouble from the Suts, aren't you, Mr. Slocum?" Blenstool asked.

The question irritated Slocum. Does it show that much, he asked himself. Can he read my thoughts? But he tried to keep his irritation to himself.

"This won't stop them," he said.

"No," said Blenstool. "I suppose not. One or more of them might even be aboard the train."

"Or they might follow on horseback," Slocum said. He looked out the window at the faces lining the track, watching the train pull out. Slowly it was picking up speed, moving out of Kellyville. Then he saw a face in the crowd that seemed to be looking right back at him. He recognized, or at least thought that he recognized, the clothes. The third man. The one who rode away from the fight in the valley. He also thought he recognized in the hard face the look of the family he was beginning to feel so familiar with, the look of the Suts.

5

Back in Kellyville, Pop Sut and his three remaining sons, Coy, Orvel, and Leroy, met with their cousins from the Kellyville area. Pop's cousin Harley was about Pop's age, and his sons, Corey and Hiram, were in their mid-twenties, as were Pop's boys. They were gathered around a table in the saloon there in Kellyville, sharing a bottle of rye whiskey.

"The son of a bitch killed Rhile," Pop was saying. "I don't mean to let anyone get away with killing one of my boys."

Old Harley sipped from his whiskey, smacked his lips, and looked at his cousin. "He's killed two of my boys now, Pop," he said. "I want him at least as bad as you do. I got twice as much reason."

"Numbers don't matter," Pop said. "He's killed a Sut or he's killed twenty Suts. He's got to be killed, and he's got to be killed by us. We mess around too long—a gunfighter like that—someone's going to kill him sooner or later. We got to get to him first."

"What about that eastern dude that's traveling with him?" Coy asked.

"You was there, Hiram," said Pop, turning to Coy's cousin for an answer to Coy's question. "Did that dude shoot either one of your brothers?"

"No, sir, he didn't," Hiram answered. "He was there all right, and he shot a popgun at us, but it didn't do no good. It was Slocum's rifle that did the killing."

"He's running with Slocum," Pop said, "and he tried to help him out. If he gets in our way, we'll kill him, but if he stands aside, we'll let him live. Agreed?"

The other Suts all nodded or grunted their agreement.

"Well," said Hiram, "that train's getting farther ahead of us all the time."

"Drain your glasses," said Pop, "and let's hit the trail. We can catch it at Hang Dog Pass."

Slocum watched while Blenstool slept. They had agreed that they would spell each other that way, for both men needed sleep, having been awake the whole night before. Even so, Slocum knew that he couldn't sleep—not yet—so he had told the detective to get the first round of shut-eye.

He had seen no one on the train that had that Sut look, but that didn't really mean anything. Most any family had someone with a stray look among them. And the one that he had recognized back in Kellyville had not gotten on the train. He knew that. But even that didn't mean anything. Someone else could be on the train. It seemed more likely, though, that the clan was planning to follow the train. There were always places where trains had to slow, steep grades and such, and trains had to stop to take on water and wood. They also made scheduled stops to pick up and let off passengers and baggage.

Determined men mounted on good horses could catch up somewhere along the way. And Slocum figured that was the way the attack would come—from horseback. Even so, he didn't relax. Logic was one thing. But there could still be a Sut on the train. He watched everyone who moved through the car.

Damn me for a chivalrous fool, he thought, and he could feel the effects of a sleepless night catching up with him. He wasn't afraid that he would drop off. He knew that he could keep himself awake. But he did have a groggy feeling, and it was enough that, if confronted with a surprise problem like the sudden appearance of a Sut, he would not be as fast as he would otherwise. Well, in a while Blenstool would wake up and Slocum could grab a nap. He hoped that nothing would happen in the meantime. He thought that it probably would not.

Slocum dreamed of the Lady Eve. He was sitting in a beautifully appointed room in a plush chair, puffing on an expensive cigar. His right hand held a large brandy snifter which was half filled with expensive bourbon. And then she swept into the room, moving as if on air, and suddenly, magically, she was in his arms, and the air was filled with sweet smells.

And then they were rolling naked in each other's arms on the softest bed that Slocum had ever felt in his life. His face was buried between her lovely white breasts, and they were rolling over and over as if floating on a soft cloud high up in the sky. And then his cheek was lying against the inside of her thigh, and with both his hands he stroked her long leg.

He came awake to the lurching of the train. He sat up straight, eyes wide, looking around. Everything was as it had been before he had dropped off to sleep. Blenstool, sitting next to him, spoke without looking at him.

"We're stopping for water," the detective said.

"It could happen here," Slocum said.

"If they should come aboard," said Blenstool, "and start shooting in this car, innocent people could be hurt."

"Let's go outside," said Slocum.

The two got out of their seats and moved to the door at the end of the car. Another lurch or two and the train came to a stop. Slocum paused in the doorway, looking around for any signs of danger. Then he dropped to the ground. Blenstool followed him. A man on top of the water tank was lowering the long snout down to give the great engine a long drink.

Slocum walked out a distance from the tracks looking around at the landscape. Blenstool followed him. A rifle shot's distance away the ground began to rise slowly and gradually to gentle, tree-covered hills. Slocum and Blenstool walked back to the train and moved between two cars to check the other side. It was quiet there, too, and they could see for a long ways uninterrupted. There was nothing but flat plain. Slocum gestured toward the top of a boxcar.

"Up there?" Blenstool asked.

"We'll have a hell of a view," said Slocum.

They walked to the car, and, as Slocum started climbing, the conductor trotted toward them.

"Here!" he shouted. "What do you think you're doing?"

"Just being careful," said Slocum, looking down from the ladder.

"Conductor," said Blenstool, speaking confidentially, "we have reason to believe that this train may be attacked. This seems a likely place."

The conductor stammered and finally said, "Well, what are they after?"

"Me," said Slocum, and he climbed on up to the top of the car. Blenstool put a comforting hand on the nervous conductor's shoulder.

"Just keep calm," he said, flashing some kind of identification under the conductor's eyes. "We're watching for them. I'm a private detective. Don't say anything to cause a panic among the passengers."

"No. No. Of course not," said the conductor, and he started sweeping the horizon with nervous eyes. Blenstool followed Slocum to the top of the car.

"See anything?" he asked.

"Nothing so far," said Slocum.

"Maybe they're not coming."

"Or maybe they just ain't caught up with us yet."

"Yeah," said Blenstool. "Maybe."

Blenstool watched the empty plain on the one side while Slocum kept his attention on the wooded hillside on the other. The thirsty engine still drank water. Steam hissed, and the idling engine chugged. Below, the nervous conductor seemed to look in all directions at once. Then Blenstool touched Slocum lightly on the shoulder, at the same time taking his Webley out of his pocket.

"Right behind us," he said.

Slocum turned to look back down the track. Seven riders were coming.

"Suts?" said Blenstool.

"That's likely," said Slocum. "Come on."

They climbed back down the ladder and started running toward the caboose. Blenstool shouted over his shoulder to the conductor as he ran.

"Keep everyone on board the train," he said.

"Yes, sir," the conductor said.

Back at the caboose, two railroad workers were lounging on the platform on the back of the car.

"Get inside," said Slocum.

They looked at the two men with guns in their hands and then down the track at the approaching seven riders. Both men tried to get into the car through the door at the same time. Blenstool leaned against the side of the caboose on the right side while Slocum moved on to the left. They waited until the riders were close enough to understand a shout.

"Hold it," Slocum called out. The riders pulled up. "Are you Suts?"

"We're Suts!" shouted Pop. "You Slocum?"

"That's right," Slocum said. "One of you ride up here and let's talk."

"There ain't nothing to talk about, Slocum," Pop said. "We come to kill you."

"Rhile shot first," Slocum said. "I had no choice. And those other two bushwhacked us. You're running me out of the county. Why don't we just leave it at that?"

"We can't do that, Slocum," said Pop. "You've killed Suts, and we got to kill you. Tell that little eastern dude with you that he can get back on the train and mind his own business. We got no quarrel with him."

"You heard him, Blenstool," Slocum said. "No need for you to get yourself killed over this."

"Sut!" Blenstool yelled. "I'm a private detective. My job is to take Mr. Slocum back to St. Louis with me, and I intend to do it. If you want Mr. Slocum, you'll have to go through me first."

"Now you've done it, you silly little shit," said Slocum, but inside he was grateful for Blenstool's stance. He needed all the help he could get.

"You want to get yourself killed," Pop Sut shouted, "we'll gladly oblige! Come on, boys."

Pop pulled out his revolver and spurred his horse, whooping and racing toward the caboose. The other six Suts followed his example. Three wild shots spanged against metal. Slocum ducked beneath the corner of the caboose and lined up for a shot at Pop. Blenstool waited patiently, still leaning against the opposite side of the car. The Suts fanned out, Pop and his boys headed for Slocum's side of the car, Hiram and his sons riding around on the other side. Riding fast, Hiram got out ahead, and Blenstool dropped him from the saddle with one shot.

An instant later Slocum fired, and his shot tore into the chest of old Pop Sut. Pop roared, dropped his gun and the reins to his mount. He clutched at the saddle horn with both hands, and the frightened horse began jumping around. Pop fell, landing hard like a sack of flour.

Coy and Orvel rode past Slocum before they could slow their horses and turn them. As they did, Coy shouted, "He got Pop!" Leroy had managed to slow his mount sooner, and he jumped down out of the saddle and ran to his father's side. "Pop," he said. "Pop." As he knelt by his dead father's side, Leroy fired a shot at Slocum. It went wide. Slocum took his time and sent a slug into Leroy's chest. Leroy jerked, groaned, and fell across the body of old Pop.

Harley and Coy, on the other side of the tracks, had turned their horses and raced back away from the train to a safe distance. They watched, helpless, as Pop's last two sons, Coy and Orvel, lashed their mounts, headed for Slocum again. Slocum stood up and leveled his Colt at Coy. He knew he could drop him. He didn't know if Orvel would get a good shot off at him in the same time or not. The two riders came closer, shouting and firing wildly as they rode.

They were close enough, Slocum decided. He really couldn't afford to let them get closer. He squeezed the trigger and Coy jerked in the saddle. Just then Blenstool stepped up beside Slocum and fired the Webley, knocking Orvel from his horse's back. Coy still reeled in the saddle, his confused horse walking this way and that. At last Coy fell to the ground. He moved no more.

Slocum and Blenstool, revolvers still in hand, looked back down the track to where Harley and Corey sat on their horses watching. They glanced around at the bodies to make sure no one was moving. All five seemed to be dead. At least, none of them showed any movement. They looked again toward Harley and Corey.

"What now?" Slocum shouted.

"Slocum!" Harley shouted back. "Can I ride up and talk?"

"You had your chance for that," Slocum said.

"That was my brother answered you back then," Harley said. "This is me."

He pulled the rifle from his saddle boot and handed it to Corey. Then he unbuckled the belt from around his waist and gave it over to his son. He held his arms out to his sides. "I ain't armed now, Slocum," he called.

"Come on over," said Slocum. He walked away from the caboose to meet Harley Sut. Blenstool had taken up his original spot beside the caboose and waited and watched, his Webley in hand. As Harley came close to Slocum, he halted his horse.

"It's over, Slocum," Harley said. "If you're willing. My brother and all his boys is dead, and I've just got one son left to me. I don't want to see him dead, too."

"I never wanted this fight in the first place," Slocum said.

"Can I pick up—my family?"

Slocum sighed. He made a gesture toward Corey.

"Ride back there with your boy and wait," Slocum said. "When this train is out of sight, do whatever you want. But I'll be watching as long as I can see you."

6

From the rear of the caboose, Slocum and Blenstool watched the remaining Suts as long as they could. The two just sat there on their horses staring after the train. In a way, Slocum thought, in spite of himself, it was a sad scene. He couldn't be sure, of course, but he thought that old Harley had probably meant it when he had said that it was over. His weathered old face had worn a long, hangdog look. He seemed whipped in more ways than one, there with his one remaining son in the midst of the bodies of his son, his brother, and his nephews. The two figures grew smaller and smaller and at last faded from view in the distance.

When they had left the Suts well behind, Slocum and Blenstool made their way back to the passenger car and settled back down in their same seats, considerably more relaxed than they had been since they had first pulled out of Frogtown hurriedly in the middle of the night, watching over their shoulders. Somehow that seemed like a long time back, Slocum thought.

"You believe him?" Blenstool asked.

"Sut?"

"Yes. Do you believe that it's over with them?"

"I tend to," said Slocum, scrunching down farther in his seat.

"Just the same," said the detective, "I shall remain vigilant."

"Good idea," said Slocum. He pulled his hat down low in front and closed his eyes, hoping that he could find his way back into the same dream he had left before. Instead he found himself in the middle of a ferocious gun battle. He had no idea how long he had been asleep, when he felt himself being jostled back to the real world. He blinked and rubbed his eyes with the back of his hand. It was Blenstool shaking him awake.

"What is it?" he asked, and his hand went automatically to the handle of his Colt.

"Sorry," the detective said. "I didn't mean to startle you. There's no problem. I don't know about you, but I'm about to starve, and I don't want to leave you here alone. Just in case. Besides, your sleep didn't seem to be entirely restful. Will you join me for a meal in the dining car? It's on the expense account, of course."

"Yeah," said Slocum. "Sure. Now that you mention it, I could use a feed. And you were right about the sleep. It wasn't worth a damn."

Getting up, they made their way through three passenger cars to the plush dining car. It looked for all the world like one of the fanciest restaurants Slocum had ever seen. Only about half the tables were occupied, for it wasn't really mealtime. Slocum and Blenstool sat across from each other at a table beside a window. The table was covered with a white linen cloth, and cloth napkins were nattily peaked beside place settings. A waiter appeared almost as soon as they were seated. He placed a menu on the table in front of each man.

"May I get you gentlemen drinks while you study the menu?" he asked.

Slocum ordered his favorite bourbon. He felt like he

needed a drink, and he thought he damn well deserved it, too. He noticed that Blenstool ordered black coffee. Well, hell, he thought, that's his own damn business. Looking over the bill of fare, Slocum said, "Hell, I don't even know what half of this damn stuff is." When the very proper waiter returned with the drinks, Slocum ordered a steak and potatoes. Blenstool had quail and some vegetables that Slocum didn't even recognize on the plate. The food was good, though. Slocum had to admit that. Their meal done, Slocum ordered himself another whiskey. After all, he reminded himself, everything was paid for by Blenstool's expense account. Slocum hadn't wanted to make this trip in the first place. Now that he was on his way, he decided that he should take full advantage of the situation.

Even though both men believed that Harley Sut had been telling them the truth when he had said that the fight between the Suts and Slocum was over and done, they were still a little edgy. They looked over the faces in the dining car for any potential danger.

There was no agreement between them to do this, but each man could tell that the other was also studying faces. They saw no one that looked like a Sut to them, no one with any particularly suspicious look, no seeming threats. There were a few old men and women, one young couple, and one big man in a tight suit, who looked to Slocum like an eastern dude.

Slocum chuckled to himself at that thought, remembering his first impression of Blenstool. The dude across the way was bigger and looked a lot tougher than the little detective, but even Blenstool had proved himself to be worthwhile in a scrap. Slocum reminded himself to try in the future not to be so quick to judge a man by the cut of his clothes. He dismissed the thought and finished his drink.

"Have another?" Blenstool asked.

"No, thanks," said Slocum. Things seemed calm enough, but he wasn't yet totally relaxed, and he wasn't ready to be. "That's enough for now."

They got up to leave the dining car, Blenstool in the lead, and the man Slocum had noticed earlier, "the eastern dude" seated at the table on the other side of the car, quickly drained his coffee cup, stood up, tossed his money on the table, and followed them.

He was, as Slocum had noted, a big man, dressed in the manner of the cities. His suit seemed to fit him a bit too tightly, and he was clean shaven. He wore no hat on his head. A closer look than Slocum had taken would have revealed large, hard-looking hands, toughened either by hard work or by fighting or by both.

He followed Blenstool and Slocum through the first car. Then Blenstool moved through the door and out onto the lurching platform between cars. The man in the tight suit moved faster. Blenstool opened the next door and stepped into the next car just as Slocum stepped through the first door. Withdrawing a blackjack from his jacket pocket, the stranger moved quickly up behind Slocum, raising his arm over his head.

They were on the jerking platform between two cars when the stranger swung his blackjack. At just the right instant the train lurched around a curve in the tracks, and the blackjack only caught Slocum a glancing blow on the side of his head. That was bad enough. He saw stars and staggered. He was weak and dizzy. His knees buckled as he turned to face his unknown attacker in a futile attempt to defend himself against this sudden, totally unexpected surprise attack.

The stranger raised his arm to swing again, and Slocum managed to ward off the blow with his own left arm. He grabbed for the stranger, and they wrestled back and forth on the unstable platform, from one car door to the other. Slocum was still reeling dizzily from the blow to his head, and the big stranger outweighed him considerably. He felt himself pushed hard against the door, and then the stranger managed to jerk his right arm loose. He raised it high overhead for another blow with the blackjack.

Then the door behind him opened and Blenstool came out. The detective grabbed the stranger's arm, and the big man turned to face this new and unexpected threat. Released suddenly, Slocum slipped to the lurching floor of the platform. The stranger's weight bore Blenstool back to the door opposite Slocum. Slocum struggled to his feet as the stranger smacked Blenstool across the face with his left.

He was about to deal another blow, when Slocum grabbed him from behind, and with a mighty effort, jerked him away from Blenstool. The stranger staggered back against the rail. The train gave another lurch, and the stranger flew back over the rail with a scream.

Together, Slocum and Blenstool looked over the edge of the rail and watched, fascinated, as the man hit the ground with a thud and bounced a couple of times. As the train carried them quickly away from the scene, the stranger seemed to be lying still. The attacker long gone from their sight, two men looked at each other.

"Do you suppose the fall killed him?" Blenstool asked.

"If not," said Slocum, "it sure as hell knocked him silly."

"At any rate," said Blenstool, "I don't think he'll bother us again."

Slocum thought again about his initial reaction to both "eastern dudes," Blenstool and the stranger. He glanced at Blenstool, and he noticed a dark bruise on the side of the detective's face. The man had dealt him a hell of a blow, and the little "eastern dude" had stood up to it. Even more important, though, the detective had once again saved Slocum's hide.

Back in the passenger car, Blenstool and Slocum resumed their seats. Slocum looked again at the ugly bruise on the detective's face. "You okay?" he asked. "That's a dandy lump you got."

"Oh, yes," said Blenstool, gingerly touching the sore spot on his jaw. "I'm just fine. I've been hit harder than that before—any number of times. It's an occupational hazard, and one gets used to it. Sort of. I wonder who that man was anyway?"

"That's what I've been thinking about," Slocum said.

"The Suts again?"

"Maybe," said Slocum, "but I don't think so. He didn't look like them."

"No," said Blenstool. "And it didn't hardly seem their style, either. Did it?"

"I didn't really have time to get a good look at the bastard," Slocum said, "only across the dining room, but from the way he was dressed, I don't even think he's from these parts."

"Oh, I agree," Blenstool said. "I also noticed him back there in the dining car. I had him figured from the first as a city dweller, and because of that, I didn't even consider that he would be a problem."

"Yeah," Slocum muttered. The attack had him, if not worried, at least perplexed. He had certainly been attacked often enough in his life, but he usually knew why, and he usually knew who the attacker was. The stranger in the tight suit was a real puzzle.

"He might have just meant to rob you," Blenstool said.

"Yeah," said Slocum. "Maybe."

"That type is common in the cities, and they do ride the

rails looking for victims. I've heard of it before, more than once.''

''I wouldn't know about that,'' Slocum said. ''But if I was looking over the passengers on this train for someone to rob, I'd pick on you before I would me. You or several others. Do I look to you like I'd be carrying a lot of money on me, or a fancy watch or something?''

Blenstool smiled. ''Now that you mention it,'' he said, ''I see your point. And I agree, but what then? If not the Suts and not a common robbery attempt, what was it?''

Slocum glanced at the city detective, noting the style of his dress, and he thought about the stranger they had thrown overboard. The two men sure as hell looked as if they came from the same world. And it wasn't Slocum's world. But the man had attacked Slocum, not Blenstool. Slocum shoved his hat back and scratched his head.

''I don't know,'' he said, and he really didn't know.

7

St. Louis was much worse than anything Slocum had imagined it would be. Getting off the train at the depot, he thought he had never heard such racket, never seen so many people in one place, never experienced such mass confusion. People were running in every direction and shouting. There was a tremendous rush on the lunch counter with men shoving women and children out of the way in their hurry to get a meal before their train pulled out.

Once or twice Slocum thought about grabbing one of the uncouth bastards and knocking him on his ass, but he reminded himself that, but for his chivalry, he would still be relaxing in Frogtown, perhaps in the company of the lovely Lady Eve. He clenched his teeth and looked the other way.

Besides, he told himself, he had to keep his eye on Blenstool. If the little detective got ahead of him in the crowd, Slocum might wander aimlessly in the big city never to find his way out again. He felt more helpless than he could remember having felt. He was completely out of his element and therefore totally dependant on Blenstool. A hell of a situation to be in, he thought, and he wondered why he had let himself get into this mess. True, he had needed to escape Frogtown in a hurry, but he could have as easily ridden away alone. Why, oh, why, he asked himself, did he ride out with the detective?

With Blenstool's very capable assistance, Slocum located a stable near the depot and boarded his horse. It occurred to him that he ought to simply mount up and head west, but he had got in this deep. He might as well see it through. Blenstool paid the stable man, and Slocum followed him back out onto the busy street, where the little man waved an arm. A carriage pulled over and stopped. Blenstool gestured for Slocum to climb in. Then he followed, and leaning forward, he spoke to the driver.

"Wellington Hotel," he said.

The driver snapped the reins, and the carriage jerked forward. Soon it settled into a smooth ride. The driver was skillful, and his gray mare trotted handsomely down the street. But the street was full of traffic, other carriages, freight wagons, pedestrians, men on horseback. More than once, Slocum thought that they were about to be involved in a terrible collision with another rig, but the driver managed to weave his way in and out of the road mess.

They passed a fistfight on the sidewalk, and in another block Slocum noticed a policeman standing against a storefront with his arms folded over his chest, casually looking out on the melee in front of him. Slocum had thought that perhaps things would settle down a bit once they had left the depot behind. He was about to decide that he had been sadly mistaken, that the only way to get any peace and quiet again would be to get the hell out of this city.

Then the driver made a turn, and suddenly they were riding down a much quieter street. Slocum breathed a sigh of relief. Another few blocks, the driver pulled up in front of the biggest, fanciest building Slocum had ever seen. WELLINGTON was carved into the stone over the front door. A long and wide canvas awning covered the sidewalk in front of the entrance, which was tended by a man in a uniform. Slocum thought that it was a silly-looking suit, and he wondered how much money they had to pay the man to get him to wear it.

Blenstool dismounted, took out some money, and paid the driver. "Keep it," he said, and the driver thanked him. Slocum came down, and the driver snapped the reins and drove away. Slocum looked up at the high building and wondered again just what the hell he was doing there.

"Well," said Blenstool, "this is the place. Come along."

Slocum followed the detective through the big front doors into the large, open hotel lobby. They walked across the marble floor to the highly polished oak counter.

"This is Mr. Slocum," Blenstool said to the dapper clerk. "I believe you're expecting him."

The clerk flipped through some cards.

"Ah, yes," he said. "One of Mr. Lewes's clients." He dipped a pen in an inkwell and held it out for Slocum. "Would you just sign the registry, sir?" he asked. Slocum took the pen and signed, then laid it down. The clerk placed a key on the counter in front of him.

"Number twelve," he said. "First floor at the top of the stairs, about halfway down the hall on the right."

"Thanks," said Slocum.

"I'll walk up with you," Blenstool said. "When you've put your things away, I'd like to introduce you to Mr. Lewes."

They mounted the long, wide stairway and came to a hallway of plush carpet. Slocum didn't like the feel of walking on the soft surface. He was overwhelmed when he unlocked the door to number twelve and stepped inside. He had never been in a fancier room in a whorehouse.

"You sure this ain't a mistake?" he said, looking at Blenstool.

The detective shook his head and smiled. "There's no mistake," he said. "This is your room. There's a restaurant downstairs and a bar. Anything you want, just sign for it, for as long as you're here.''

"I don't like sponging off of this lawyer Lewes," Slocum said. "Hell, I don't even know him."

"It's your uncle's money that's paying for all this," Blenstool said. "Not Mr. Lewes's. By the way, shall we go meet him? Mr. Lewes, that is."

Slocum glanced around the room, shrugged, and tossed his blanket roll on the bed. "Let's go," he said.

Back downstairs Blenstool made an inquiry at the desk, then returned to Slocum and led the way into the bar. Like everything else about the Wellington, the bar was elegant. Blenstool looked around until his eyes lighted on a man sitting alone at a table with a bottle and a glass in front of him. He led Slocum over to that table, and the man stood as he saw them approaching.

"Blenstool," he said, extending his hand.

The detective shook the man's hand, then nodded at Slocum.

"Mr. Lewes," he said, "this is John Slocum. Mr. Slocum, Mr. Lewes."

Lewes pumped Slocum's hand. "Glad to see you," he said. "Very glad. We couldn't move forward here without you. Sit down, gentlemen. Sit down."

"Excuse me," said Blenstool. "My job here is done. I'll just be on my way." He touched the brim of his derby, then turned to Slocum. "It's been very interesting, Mr. Slocum," he said.

"Where you off to, Blenstool?" Lewes asked.

"I was promised a vacation after this job," the detective said. "I think I'll make a run to a place called Frogtown. I left some unfinished business there."

Slocum smiled. "Have fun," he said.

Blenstool left the bar, and Slocum and Lewes sat down at the table. Lewes motioned for a waiter.

"What'll you have, Mr. Slocum?" he asked.

Slocum looked at the bottle on the table. It was a fine Kentucky bourbon. "That right there looks good to me," he said.

The waiter came over to the table, and Lewes called for another glass. When it arrived, he poured Slocum a drink. Slocum lifted the glass and took half of it in a swallow.

"Thanks," he said. He looked over the glass at the lawyer across the table from him. A man about his own age, the lawyer was dressed in what Slocum figured was an expensive city suit, but it had a rumpled, disheveled look about it. It didn't seem to be the fault of the suit, though. The man looked as if he could put on a brand-new, tailored suit of clothes and still look rumpled.

The thinning, reddish hair on his head poked out here and there in directions it shouldn't have, and his face was red. It had the look of the face of a man who drank too much whiskey. Slocum liked his whiskey as well as the next man, but there were some folks who just couldn't take it. He knew that. Lewes seemed to be one of those men.

Oh, he didn't seem drunk. He might drink all day long and not show it in that way. But it showed in the ruddiness of his face, and in the fine red lines that wandered around his bulbous nose. Slocum had known men like that before, and he knew the look. He drained his glass of whiskey, and Lewes poured him a refill.

"You look like a man of the West, Slocum," the lawyer said.

"I been out West since the end of the war," Slocum said.

"I trust you had a good trip back here with Blenstool."

"Well," Slocum said, "it was interesting."

"I, uh, I suppose," Lewes said, "you'll be anxious to see all your relatives again."

"I don't know them," Slocum said. "Hell, I don't hardly recall old Ferdie. I can't believe he'd want to be leaving anything to me. I never even thought that he liked me. I don't really know what the hell I'm doing here."

Lewes poured himself another drink and slugged it down.

"You're here," he said, "because Ferdinand's will is explicit in insisting that all of his living heirs be present at the reading. If anyone's missing, I can't even break the seal on the document. I've told everyone else what I'm about to tell you. I don't know that he left you a dime. On the other hand, he might have left you a whopping fortune. We won't know until everyone's here and we read the will."

"You mean there's still some that ain't here?" Slocum asked.

"Sarl Diglo has not arrived as yet," said Lewes, "but we're expecting him any day now."

"I never heard that name before," Slocum said. He reached into his pocket for a cigar and a match.

"Well," the lawyer said, "he's an heir. A relative of yours. Distant cousin or something. Everything's verified. We know for sure that we've located all the living heirs, and we know that they're all legitimate."

Slocum sent up a puff of smoke. "What the hell was that name again?" he asked.

"Diglo," said Lewes. "Sarl Diglo."

Slocum shook his head. "It don't mean a thing to me," he said. "Hell, it don't even sound real."

"It is an unusual name," the lawyer said. "That seems to have been a habit with your family. Unusual names. Your own is about the most common we've run across."

Slocum took another sip of whiskey and raised an eyebrow as he spotted a lovely young woman walk into the room, stop, and look around. She wore a fancy ruffled dress with a long, full skirt. Even so, he could tell that underneath it she had a shapely body. Her hair was long, curly, and blond and framed a smooth face with a turned-up nose and full, rosy lips. She spotted Lewes and headed directly for the table where Slocum and the lawyer sat. As she came close, Slocum stood and removed his hat. She seemed to ignore him.

"Mr. Lewes," she said. "I'm so glad to find you here. A lady should never sit alone in a saloon."

"Please join us," said Lewes. "Miss Bloe, this is a cousin of yours, John Slocum. Slocum, this is Miss Demmi Bloe."

Slocum pulled out a chair for Miss Bloe. She looked at him, smiled and sat down. He scooted her chair forward a little for her, then resumed his own seat.

"Glad to know you, ma'am," he said.

"Oh, please," she said. "Don't 'ma'am' your own cousin. Call me Demmi. May I call you John?"

"Sure," he said. "So—you're my cousin."

"I'd say second or third cousin," Lewes said, "once or twice removed. I can't remember all the details, but it's not too close. Still, you are related, and you're both heirs of Ferdinand. What are you drinking, Miss Bloe? Chablis, as usual?"

"Yes," she said. "Thank you."

Lewes waved an arm for a waiter, but Slocum wasn't paying any attention to the lawyer. He was looking over his newly found cousin, and he couldn't help noticing the way she looked back at him. He was glad to know that the relationship was not a very close one, the family relationship, that is. He did have another kind of relationship in mind. For the first time since he had met Blenstool back in

Frogtown, he was almost glad to be involved in this silly mess.

"You look like a cowboy," Demmi said.

"Well, I have punched a few cows," Slocum admitted, "but I try not to do it too regular."

"Oh? But you are a westerner?"

"That's right."

The waiter came and Lewes ordered Demmi's wine. The waiter hustled away to fill the order. Demmi was still gazing at Slocum.

"What do you do for a living, John?" she asked.

"Oh, I'll work at most anything that comes along," Slocum said. "For a while."

"I understand from Blenstool," Lewes said, "that you've been known as a hired gun."

Slocum sipped from his whiskey. "I've done that kind of work," he said.

"A gunfighter," Demmi said. "That's exciting. I had no idea there was a gunfighter in the family. All the rest are so—well, ordinary."

"Well," Slocum said, "I ain't really been part of any family for a good long time."

The waiter returned with a small wineglass and a carafe. He poured Demmi a glass and stood by while she tasted it.

"Lovely," she said. The waiter made a curt bow and disappeared. "Thank you, Mr. Lewes," she added.

"No thanks necessary, Miss Bloe," Lewes said. "The one thing your uncle left that was not sealed in the will was the money to cover this gathering and instructions that you're all to be well taken care of. Along with my fee, of course."

He stood up and waved at the waiter, catching his attention, then he grabbed up the bottle on the table by its neck. He held it up. "Bring another one of these," he said. Then he looked down at Slocum and Demmi. "I'm turning in. Slocum, if want to join us in the dining room in the morning around nine, you'll get a chance to meet the others. All those who're here already." He said good night and left the bar.

The waiter brought a fresh bottle to the table, and Slocum opened it and poured himself another drink. He noticed that Demmi's glass was empty, so he reached for her carafe. She smiled and pushed her glass toward him. "Yes, please," she said.

8

It was getting late, and Slocum thought that he'd had enough whiskey anyhow, so he excused himself, telling Demmi that he was going to call it a night. As he shoved back his chair to stand, his lovely cousin downed what was left of her wine in a swallow.

"Me, too," she said. "It is getting late, and I'm just a little bit woozy. Walk me to my room—cousin?"

Slocum stepped around behind her and pulled out her chair as she stood.

"Sure," he said.

Together they left the bar, crossed the big lobby, and mounted the stairs. About halfway up, Demmi paused. She put the back of her wrist to her forehead, swayed slightly, and exhaled out loud.

"Oh, my," she said. "I must have overdone it just a wee bit."

Slocum put an arm around her waist for support.

"You going to make it?" he asked.

"Yes," she said. "I think I'm all right now. Thank you. Oh, how embarrassing. I'm not used to drinking that much, you know."

"No need to be embarrassed, ma'am, uh, Demmi," said Slocum. "Hell, I've been known to be falling down drunk a time or two myself."

"Why," Demmi protested, "I'm not—"

"No," Slocum said quickly. "I didn't mean that the way it sounded, I guess. I just meant that I've been there, and so after the little you had, you sure don't need to feel embarrassed about it. Not around me anyhow. That's all I meant. Come on now."

They walked the rest of the way up the stairs and started down the hallway. Demmi stopped at a door, opened up her purse, and pulled out a key. She dangled it in front of Slocum.

"This is my room," she said.

Slocum took the key and opened the door. Then he handed the key back to Demmi and touched the brim of his hat.

"Good night," he said. "It's been a pleasure getting to know you."

He started to turn and walk toward his own room, but Demmi stopped him.

"You want to get to know me better?" she asked.

Slocum cocked his head and looked at her, his eyes squinty.

"Come in," she said. "I don't want to be alone."

Slocum looked up and down the hallway, feeling somehow that some discretion was called for. No one was anywhere in sight, so he stepped quickly inside Demmi's room and pulled the door shut behind himself. Demmi held the key out toward him again. A suggestive look was on her lovely face. Slocum took the key and locked the door.

When he turned back around, she had stepped up close. She was right there, and he had turned into her arms. She pulled him close, mashing her soft breasts against his chest, and her head tilted back.

She looked up into his face with half-closed eyes, and her wet lips parted slightly. Slocum took the hint and pressed his mouth against hers. He had heard of kissing cousins before, but he had never thought that he'd run into one of his own. And Demmi was delightful.

Her right hand reached around behind his head, pulling it closer and tighter, tangling in his hair, and her tongue shot out suddenly and began probing the inside of his mouth. Like a snake, he thought. A lovely, wicked snake. He let her probe awhile before he jammed his own down into her waiting mouth, and then he felt her lips tighten as she sucked on it, sucked as if she might get something out of it. At last they parted, and Demmi gasped for breath.

It was dark in the room except for the moonlight streaming in through the window, and Demmi turned and moved toward the bed. Looking over her shoulder, she twisted her arms behind her back to reach for the laces that held her dress together. Slocum stepped up behind her and took over the job. Soon she was shoving the dress down toward the floor to step out of it.

By the time she was completely undressed, so was Slocum. He was standing at the foot of the bed, his rod standing out at attention. Demmi's eyes fell on it and opened wide. She stepped forward and gripped it hard, then used it like a handle or a leash to lead him into bed. It throbbed and jumped in her hand, but she held tight to keep it in her control.

She went headfirst onto the mattress, on one hand and her knees. The other hand still held his cock and pulled him after her. Slocum got a good look at her smooth, round ass before she turned over onto her back. She spread her legs and pulled his cock toward her gaping cunt.

He crawled between her legs, and she carefully placed the head of his cock between the warm, wet pussy lips, running it up and down, from top to bottom several times before aiming it into the hole. Having placed it just right, she arched, shoving her crotch up at him, and he responded by driving down. His first thrust went in hard and deep, and she gasped out loud.

He drove hard and fast then, until he was almost out of breath. Then he lowered his body completely down against her, and she raised her legs to wrap them around his waist, locking her feet together just at the small of his back.

They rocked together then more slowly and gently, and they kissed and dueled with their tongues at the same time. Slocum turned his head to kiss her neck, and he tasted the salty sweat of her body, and he liked the taste.

"Oh," she moaned. "Oh, Johnny. Oh, it's so good. Oh, oh, oh."

Then Slocum felt the pressure building, and gradually he increased his speed, and she responded. He drove harder and faster, until his crotch was pounding almost viciously against hers.

"Ah, ah, ah."

"Oh, oh, oh."

Then he felt the dam burst, and he drove hard and deep a few more thrusts before shoving into her as far as he could and holding it there as the last few spurts shot into her depths.

"Oh, Johnny," she said. "Oh, that was a gusher."

Slocum relaxed for a moment, his full weight pressing Demmi down into the mattress beneath her. Then he backed out of her slowly and rolled over onto his back. She turned and put a hand on his chest, playing with the hair that grew there. She kissed his ear and tickled it with her tongue.

"I'm glad we got acquainted," she whispered.

Slocum thought better of it, but against his own judgment, he went down to breakfast with the clan that was gathered there with Lawyer Lewes. When he saw them, he started to turn around and go the other way, but Lewes had already spotted him.

"Slocum," Lewes called out. "I'm glad you made it. Come on over and meet the others."

Lewes stood up as Slocum moved toward the long table.

"Ladies and gentlemen," Lewes said, "let me have your attention, please. I'd like to present Mr. John Slocum, from the West. He's one of you."

Lewes pulled out an empty chair which was just beside his own place at the table, and Slocum stepped around it, ready to sit down.

"Mr. Slocum," Lewes said, "these are all your relatives. I believe you've already met Miss Bloe."

Slocum looked at Demmi, across the table from his place, and touched the brim of his hat.

"Good morning, John," she said, a smile on her lips.

God, Slocum thought, anyone could read that smile.

"This is Pug Kolp," said Lewes, indicating a sallow-complected young man sitting just to Demmi's right.

"Howdy," said Slocum.

"Cousin," said Kolp, a half smile on his thin face.

"Sten Comlo," Lewes continued, "Spig Bowlig, Kirt Nerlcut, Romp Casro."

After the "Howdies" and "How do you do's" were all done, Slocum sat down. He was thinking that his own name, which he always considered a bit unusual, was normal compared to these others, and he was wondering just what kind of family he had come from. He decided right away that he had made the right choice when he had become a lone wolf, wandering the West with no other company than his big 'paloose. And he told himself that he had already had more than enough of this family—well, of all but one anyhow.

"Well," said Cousin Comlo, "at least Uncle Ferdie has one Slocum left among his heirs."

Slocum grunted. He couldn't think of anything to say to that comment. Lewes flagged a waiter, who came to the table quickly.

"The rest of us have ordered," the lawyer said.

Slocum put in an order for ham and eggs, and the waiter hurried away toward the kitchen.

"Are you a cowpuncher, Mr. Slocum?" Spig Bowlig asked.

"I have been," said Slocum. "It's not my favorite line of work."

"Awfully smelly, I would imagine," said Kolp.

Slocum looked hard at the cynical young man across the table.

"I've run across worse stinks," he said.

"Well, then," said Romp Casro, who all of a sudden reminded Slocum of the man he and Blenstool had thrown off the train, "if you ain't a cowpuncher, then what do you do out there in the West? Kill Indians?"

"Why would I want to kill Indians?" Slocum asked. And silently he asked himself, Can I really be related to these assholes?

"I noticed that gun you're wearing," said Casro.

"Well?" Slocum said.

"Well, is it for show, or do you use it?"

"I've used it," Slocum said.

"Have you killed anyone?" Casro asked.

"I have."

"Well, who were they?"

Slocum put his arms on the table, leaning toward Casro.

"Mr.—what was your name?" he asked.

"Casro. They call me Romp."

"Well, Rump," said Slocum, "I don't feel near close

enough to you or the rest of this family to answer that kind of question. I'll tell you this much. They were white."

"Oh, Lord," said Kolp, the cynic, "a killer in the family. Do they call you 'shootist' out West, or is it 'gunfighter'?"

"Mostly folks just call me Slocum," said Slocum, "at least—to my face."

"Watch out, Pug," said Spig Bowlig. "Don't anger our newfound cousin. He just might part your hair with a bullet."

Slocum stood up, and Lewes, sitting beside him, flinched. The waiter was making his way toward the table with a tray load of breakfasts.

"If I was to try a trick shot like that," said Slocum, "I'd likely blow your brains out by mistake. Mr. Lewes, beg your pardon, but I spotted a little place just down the street on the way in yesterday. I guess I'll just mosey down there for a bite to eat. The company might be better there. It sure as hell can't be any worse."

"But—but your breakfast has been ordered," said Lewes.

"Let Rump eat it," said Slocum, and he shoved the chair out of his way, turning to leave the room.

"It's Romp, Cowboy!" Casro shouted.

Slocum was halfway to the door when Demmi scooted her own chair back and ran after him.

"John," she called. "John, wait."

He stopped and looked over his shoulder at her. She was running toward him.

"I might be related to them," he said to her, "but I sure don't have to like them—or eat with them."

"They were awfully rude," she said. "I don't believe I care for their company, either. May I join you?"

"I don't know what kind of place we'll find," he said.

"But you said—"

"I know," said Slocum, interrupting her. "I lied."

She chuckled. "Well, we'll just take a chance together. All right?"

"Come on," he said.

The waiter had distributed all the plates but two. He looked at Demmi's place and at Slocum's, and then he looked toward Lewes, confusion on his face.

Lewes looked toward the door to see Slocum and Demmi leaving arm in arm. He shrugged, then looked back at the perplexed waiter. Then he pointed toward Romp Casro.

"Give them to Mr. Casro," he said. "He can eat it all, I think."

9

It was midmorning when Slocum again saw Lewes. They met in the middle of the lobby as Slocum was heading for the stairway. Lewes stopped him.

"Mr. Slocum," the lawyer said, "I feel I must apologize for the behavior of the others this morning."

"They're my relatives," Slocum said, "not yours. You got nothing to apologize for."

"Well," said Lewes, "I'm in charge here, and I brought everyone together. I can't help but feel responsible."

"Mr. Lewes," Slocum said, "they're a bunch of weasels, but it ain't your fault. Don't worry about me. I take care of myself pretty good."

"Two more showed up this morning," Lewes said.

"Does that mean we're going to get this damn thing over with?" asked Slocum.

"Well, not quite yet," Lewes said. "We're still waiting for one more. Mr. Sarl Diglo. As soon as he arrives, we'll take care of the reading."

"Are you sure I'm related to all these funny-name people?" Slocum asked.

"There's no doubt about it, Mr. Slocum," the lawyer assured him. "You might be pleased to know, however, that the two who came in this morning have at least slightly more normal names: Marty Bloe and Charlie Slocum."

"Well," Slocum said, "at least one of them sounds like someone who might really be family."

"Would you like to meet them?"

"Naw. It'll keep. If they're anything like the others, the less I see of them the better. Thanks anyway."

Slocum went upstairs to his room and slept. He woke up hungry, checked his pocketwatch, and found that it was well past lunchtime. Good, he thought. Maybe that crazy bunch will be done and out of the dining room. He dressed and left the room.

That night, once again, Slocum and Demmi rolled in each other's arms, this time in Slocum's room. They had just completed a magnificent fuck and were lying quietly side by side when a door banged out in the hallway, as if someone had thrown it open and swung it hard back against the wall. Then there was a sound, at once like a cry for help and a gurgling, choking sound.

Slocum jumped out of bed and pulled on his trousers. He grabbed his Colt and ran to the door, jerking it open and stepping out into the hallway. He looked first one way and then the other. Down by the head of the stairs, he saw a man swaying and clutching at his throat. Just then two more doors opened. Lewes stuck his head out of a room, and so did Casro.

"What is it?" Casro said.

"Down there," said Slocum, and he ran toward the stairs. Lewes and Casro followed. The man swayed uneasily on his feet, and just before Slocum reached him, he pitched forward, tumbling down the long stairway. Slocum followed as quickly as he could. At the foot of the stairs he turned the man over to discover that it was Pug Kolp, the cynical, smart-alecky young man from breakfast. A thin necktie was tightly knotted around his throat, but his neck was broken from the fall. He was dead.

"Good Lord," said Lewes. "It's young Kolp."

"Yeah," said Slocum. "And he's deader'n hell."

"What happened?" asked Casro.

"I don't know anymore than you do," said Slocum. "I heard a noise and came out of my room. He was standing up there." Slocum pointed toward the top of the stairs. "Before I could get to him, he fell."

The night clerk had come over by then, and Sten Comlo and Spig Bowlig were hurrying down the stairs.

"You threatened him just this morning," Casro said, accusing Slocum.

"There's no need for that," said Lewes.

"Well, he did," Casro said, "and he's a killer. He admitted it."

Lewes turned to the clerk, ignoring Casro's last remark.

"You'd better get the police," he said.

"Yes, sir," said the clerk, and he turned and ran. Lewes then turned to face Casro once again.

"I came out of my room at just about the same time Slocum came out of his," he said. "Kolp was already at the head of the stairs. I saw Slocum run to try to keep him from falling."

"Cousin Slocum," said Sten Comlo, "what happened? I mean, what do you think? Was he strangled?"

"It looks to me like someone tried to strangle him," Slocum said. "But he must have broke loose and come out in the hall looking for help. He was choked pretty good, though. He was wobbly on his feet. He fell down the stairs and broke his neck. That's what killed him."

"Was someone trying to rob him?" Bowlig asked.

Slocum stood up and started to climb the stairs.

"How would I know?" he said. He shot a glance at

Lewes. "I'm going up to get dressed. I imagine the police will be wanting to talk to all of us when they get here."

He found Demmi in the hall with her robe wrapped around her, as if she had just come out of her own room like the others.

"John?" she said.

He told her quickly what had happened and suggested she go back to her room and get dressed. She hurried down the hall. Slocum went into his room and dressed. By the time he got back down the stairs, he saw the whole family crowded around a man he had not seen before. The man was middle-aged and portly, dressed in a three-piece suit. A badge was pinned to his vest. As Slocum neared the crowd, Lewes tapped the man on his shoulder.

"Here comes Mr. John Slocum," Lewes said. "He was the first one to reach the body."

"All right," said the policeman. "The rest of you can go on back to your rooms."

The small crowd broke up, grumbling to themselves and to one another, and Slocum walked on over to join the policeman and the lawyer.

"Mr. Slocum," said Lewes, "this is the chief of police, Defe Cofy. Chief, this is John Slocum."

"A westerner?" said Cofy.

"It shows?" asked Slocum. He was getting tired of this routine.

"Tell me what happened here," said Cofy.

Slocum related the incident again.

"You heard a door slam," said Cofy, "and then you heard a choking sound?"

"That's right," said Slocum.

"You pulled on your trousers, grabbed your gun, and ran out into the hall. This jasper was standing at the head of the stairs, and he fell before you could get to him. Is that right?''

"That's what I said." Slocum tried not to let the chief see his nervousness. Lawmen always made him feel that way, but he always tried to cover it up. They already had too much of an advantage over ordinary folks. No need to give them even more.

"Well," said Cofy, "it's too bad someone didn't run directly to the victim's room. I'd say the attack took place there, and when you were running toward the stairs, the attacker was still in Mr. Kolp's room."

"Chief Cofy," Lewes said, "we all ran to see if we could help Mr. Kolp. It's only natural, I think."

"Yeah, yeah," said Cofy. "I know that. Still, I wish someone had gone to Kolp's room—or at least kept an eye on the door. Hell, it was probably a robbery attempt, and we'll most likely never solve it. Still, we'll try. Well, I guess I'm done with all of you people—at least for now. I'm going on up to Kolp's room and join my man there. If I need anything more from you, I'll let you know."

Slocum breathed a sigh of relief as Cofy headed for the stairs.

"This is awful," said Lewes. He looked at Slocum suddenly. "You, uh, you didn't do it, did you?" he asked.

Slocum grinned at the lawyer. He liked the man's direct approach.

"No," he said. "I didn't do it. I didn't like the little shit, but if I'd wanted to kill him, I'd have given him a gun and shot it out with him. Besides, I've never killed anyone just because I didn't like him. I might have called him outside and beat the shit out of him. But, no, lawyer, I didn't murder the little son of a bitch. That ain't my style."

"I didn't really think so," Lewes said. "Please forgive me, I—"

"Hell, that's all right," said Slocum. "I do have something to tell you, though."

"What is it?"

"Is that bar still open?"

"Yes," said Lewes. "I'm sure it is. Come on."

They found a table in the bar, and Lewes got them a bottle and two glasses. Seated at the table, drinks poured, they leaned conspiratorially toward each other.

"Lewes," said Slocum, "I don't know whether or not you want to pass this along to that policeman up there, but I don't think that old Kolb was killed by no thief."

"What makes you say that?" Lewes asked.

Slocum took a sip of whiskey.

"Me and Blenstool was attacked on the train on the way here," said Slocum. "Well, actually, we were attacked more than once, but I knew who the first ones was. They was the Suts, and they was after me because I'd killed one of them. But finally old Hiram Sut told us that it was all over, and I believed him. It was after that, a feller in an Eastern dude outfit jumped me from behind. He gave me a good konk on the noodle, and he was trying to do worse, when Blenstool came along and pulled him off me. The two of us kind of throwed him overboard, so we never got to question him. I never did think he was one of the Suts or that he was working for the Suts. That ain't their style, if you get my meaning."

"Yes," said Lewes, pausing to take a drink. "I think I do get your meaning."

"Blenstool said he was a city fellow," Slocum continued. "Said he'd seen a lot like him. I couldn't figure out what a city fellow would be jumping me for."

"Robbery?" Lewes asked.

"That's what Blenstool said," Slocum continued, "but I told him, if you was fixing to rob someone, and you looked at me the way I look, and you looked at your own self, which one would you pick on?''

Lewes stroked his chin and stared down at his drink on the table in front of him.

"Yes," he said. "Yes. So what we have here is we've had two attacks on the heirs of Ferdinand Slocum. One failed, and the other succeeded. The man who attacked you on the train—have you seen him again?''

"I'm not sure I'd know him if I did," said Slocum. He shoved his glass toward Lewes, who refilled it. "He hit me from behind. Blenstool might recognize him if he was to see him again, but I don't think we'll see the son of a bitch again. When we throwed him off that train, it was moving right along. If that landing didn't kill him—well, it sure as hell laid him up for a while.''

"I see," said Lewes.

Slocum took a drink, then put his glass back down.

"There's been two attacks on old Ferdie's heirs," he said. "That's for sure. But it's also damn sure that there was two different attackers. I'd bet money on that.''

Lewes finished his drink, then leaned back and scratched his head. "Slocum," he said. "Yes. Let's tell Cofy about this. What you've just told me puts a whole new light on this situation. Someone attacked you. Someone killed Kolp. If the two incidents are related, and they would seem to be, then I believe it's safe to assume that there will yet be more attacks.''

"You think old Uncle Ferdie left enough of a fortune for someone to be killing for?" Slocum asked.

Lewes shrugged. "I don't know," he said. "I really don't know. And no one else knows, either. We won't know until I open the will and read it. Perhaps someone thinks he knows. He or she.''

Slocum thought, You can't be thinking of Demmi, but

he kept his thought to himself. It had to be that someone was after the heirs, or after some of them. Nothing else made any sense. The two attacks certainly seemed to be related, and the only possible relationship was that the victims of both attacks were Ferdinand's heirs.

"So you want to tell Cofy?" Slocum asked.

"I think we should," said Lewes.

"All right," said Slocum. He downed his drink. "Let's go catch him."

They caught up with Cofy as he was coming down from his examination of Kolp's room. He had found nothing in the room to help. Slocum and Lewes told him about the attack on the train and their suspicions regarding the two attacks. Cofy looked thoughtful for a moment.

"One of your crowd," he said, looking at Slocum, "pointed a finger at you. He said that you're a notorious killer from the West, and that you threatened Mr. Kolp only this morning."

"I had words with him," said Slocum. "I didn't actually threaten the little shit."

"Well," said Cofy, "I'll look up this Blenstool in the morning and have a talk with him. If you're right about this, we're looking for someone in your group, Mr. Lewes."

"Yes," said Lewes, "I'm painfully aware of that unpleasant fact."

"Yeah," said Cofy, "well, in the meantime, get everyone down here together, over there on the far side of the lobby."

"Now?" asked Lewes.

"Right now."

10

Lawyer Lewes had all the heirs of Uncle Ferdinand Slocum gathered up in a few minutes, and Captain Cofy paced in front of them for a while, letting them get more and more nervous and fidgety. At last he stopped and stared hard at each one individually, one after the other.

"As you all know by now," he said, "one of your group, Mr. Kolp, was murdered last night."

"Are you sure then that it was a murder?" asked Sten Comlo.

"That's what I'm calling it," Cofy said. "There was a fight in his room. That's for sure. And there was an attempt to strangle him. That attempt led directly to his death from a fall down the stairs. I'm calling it murder, all right."

"Oh, dear," said Demmi.

"What was it?" asked a man Slocum had not seen before. "A robbery attempt?"

"I thought so at first," said Cofy, "but now I'm not so sure."

"Why not?" the man asked.

"There was an earlier unexplained attack on another one of your number," said Cofy. "We just found out about that."

"What?" said Nerlcut.

"Who?" asked Bowlig.

"Mr. Slocum here was attacked on his way here from the West on board the train," Cofy said.

"Did Slocum tell you that one himself?" Romp Casro asked.

"He did," said the policeman.

"Slocum's a killer," said Casro. "He's admitted it. In front of all of us. What better way for a killer to cover his tracks than to claim that he was also attacked? Or maybe I should say, what better way for him to try to cover his tracks?"

"There was a private detective with Mr. Slocum when the attack occurred," Cofy said. "I'll see him first thing in the morning to get Slocum's story confirmed."

"Or disproved," Casro added.

"That's right," said Cofy. "One way or the other. In the meantime, I see no reason to doubt the story."

"Well, I do," Casro blurted out. He stood up and turned to face Slocum, pointing an accusing finger at him. "He's an admitted killer, and he argued with Pug. The least you could do is take that gun away from him."

"No one was killed with a gun, Mr. Casro," said Lewes.

Slocum took a cigar out of his pocket and lit it with a Lucifer match. He looked through the smoke at Casro, still standing, still pointing.

"Sit down, Rump," he said. "I might kill you."

Cofy gave Slocum a look. He wondered for a moment, then shook the thought out of his head.

"Sit down, Mr. Casro," he said. "I'm handling this situation."

Casro backed toward his seat but continued pointing at Slocum.

"He just threatened me," he said. "You see? I told you he's a killer, and now he's threatened me."

"I heard him," said Cofy, "and if you don't sit down and shut up, I might threaten you myself."

Casro sat and glared at Slocum. To his right sat another man that Slocum had not seen before. Slocum figured that they were the two new arrivals Lewes had mentioned earlier. One was named Slocum and the other Bloe. He remembered that much. This one, whichever he was, leaned forward and raised his hand to get the attention of Cofy.

"Excuse me," he said.

"What?" Cofy snapped.

"I'm Martin Bloe," said the other. "I'm wondering—if Cousin Slocum's story is true—if he was attacked on his way here, and then cousin Pug was killed here, well, what does that mean?"

"I don't know what anything means, Mr. Bloe," said Cofy. "I suggest that—"

"Wait a minute," said Nerlcut, interrupting. "I get it. I know what Marty's getting at. There's no apparent connection between Slocum there and poor dead Pug. Is there any connection, Slocum?"

"I never met him or heard of him until I came here," Slocum said.

"Then the only possible connection is that which connects us all," said Nerlcut. "The fact that we're the heirs of Uncle Ferdie. And that means that someone is trying to kill us. All of us. That means that any one of us could be the next victim."

"Any one except the killer," said Bowlig.

"What?" Nerlcut asked.

"Isn't it obvious?" said Bowlig. "If someone is trying to kill all of us, then that someone has to be one of us. Who else would have a reason?"

"My God," said Nerlcut, looking from one of his relatives to another. "My God, you're right, of course. It's to eliminate the other heirs and get everything for himself."

"Or herself," said Comlo.

"Thanks, Sten," Demmi said.

"All right," said Cofy, raising his voice. "All right. So it's out in the open. It could be anyone. Or we could even be wrong about all this. It's just speculation. There might be some other explanation altogether. I suggest that you all go about your business as usual. But stay together when you can, and be sure your doors are locked at night. I'm leaving a man here with you to keep a watch. Oh, yeah. One other thing. Don't anyone try to leave town until this is all cleared up. That's all for now."

Cofy turned on his heel and headed for the front door, and it seemed to Slocum that everyone in the family group started talking at once. Slocum was sure that Romp Casro was whispering about him into the ear of Spig Bowlig, and he told himself that he didn't give a shit. Others were looking cautiously and suspiciously at one another, obviously wondering just which one of their relatives was waiting for a chance to do them in, and what the method might be, and when the attack would come.

All of a sudden Slocum found the whole thing very amusing, and he was almost glad that he had allowed Blenstool, the funny little detective, to bring him along. Then, of course, there was Demmi Bloe, his slightly more than kissing cousin. Perhaps this was better than Frogtown after all, at least for a time, and even if it wasn't better, Frogtown would still be out there later for another visit at another time. With the Sut fight called off, he could go back to Frogtown in peace. But this—this was a once-in-a-lifetime thing. And he finally admitted to himself that he was glad he wasn't missing it.

The other stranger, the one that must be the other Slocum, since Marty Bloe had identified himself, got up from his chair and walked toward Slocum. Slocum stood to meet him. He was a young man, perhaps twenty-six, and not a bad-looking fellow. Well dressed, in the city manner like the others, he was tall and straight. A pleasant smile spread across his clean-shaven face as he extended his hand.

"Hi," he said, "I'm Charlie Slocum."

"John Slocum," said Slocum, taking his newfound cousin's hand. "Glad to know you." And, though he kept the thought to himself, he was pleased that if one of this bunch had the same name as him, it was this guy. "I'm just going for a drink," he said. "Care to join me?"

"I'd be delighted," said Charlie.

Slocum glanced at Demmi, still sitting on the couch nearby.

"You want to come along?" he asked.

"I'd love to," she said, and she got up and walked into the bar with the two Slocums. Slocum called for a bottle and two glasses, and a carafe of chablis and a glass for Demmi. They found a table and sat down. In a minute the drinks were served, and the waiter left them alone.

"So," said Demmi, "there are actually two Slocums here. I think that's nice. The Slocum line has nearly vanished, you know."

"Yes," said Charlie. "It seems like a generation or two back, all the Slocum kids were female, so their kids have different names now. I'm an exception. And you, too, John, of course." He chuckled quietly. "I guess," he said, "we have a heavy responsibility, you and me. We need to bring some more male Slocums into the world before it's too late."

Charlie smiled, and Slocum raised his glass as if for a toast, then took a drink of whiskey.

"Here, here," he said.

Demmi giggled and gave Slocum a sideways glance which was not missed by Charlie.

"Say," said Slocum, changing the tone of the conversation, "I feel like a total stranger here. Kind of like a fish out of water. Do you two know all those others?"

"I do," said Demmi. "It's been a few years since I've seen most of them, but I do know them. I suppose I've known them all my life."

"I don't know them all," said Charlie, "but I remember most of them from when I was a kid."

"And Ferdinand," Slocum said. "You remember him?"

"Yes," said Charlie.

"Sure," said Demmi.

"And, uh, each other?" Slocum said.

"Why, yes," said Demmi. "Charlie and I have known each other all our lives."

"Then this whole setup," Slocum said. "It's on the level? It's real?"

Demmi and Charlie looked at each other, and they both shrugged.

"Well, yes," she said. "Sure it is. Did you think it wasn't?"

"I wasn't sure," said Slocum. "It's about the craziest thing I've ever got myself messed up in."

"If you didn't believe it was legitimate," Charlie said, "why did you come?"

Slocum ducked his head just a bit and grinned.

"I had a reason to get to somewhere," he said. "This seemed as good as any."

"Oh," said Charlie, and he blushed slightly. "I'm sorry. I didn't mean to pry into something that's none of my business."

"Hell," said Slocum. "It don't matter." He tossed down his drink and reached for the bottle. "I was taking myself a rest in a little town out West when I got myself into a scrap. Had a whole damn family after me.''

''I see,'' said Charlie. He took another cautious sip from his glass.

''A whole family,'' said Demmi. ''That sounds exciting. How many were there?''

''Ah, I don't know,'' Slocum said with a shrug. ''Six. Eight. I ain't sure.''

''Well, what happened?'' Demmi asked, leaning anxiously closer to Slocum. ''Tell me.''

''Well, that little detective had come after me,'' Slocum said, ''to bring me to this shindig. I told him to get lost, but when that family got after me, I dragged him out of bed and said let's go. We lit out, and they came after us.''

''What were they after you for in the first place?'' Demmi asked.

''Well, I'd killed one of them,'' Slocum said. ''We'd had us a fight, and it turned out he was a sore loser. He came at me with a gun, and I killed him. That's all.''

''What did you fight about?'' Demmi asked.

''You mean the fight that started the whole thing?'' Slocum asked.

''Yes. What was it over?''

''Bad manners,'' Slocum said.

Demmi cocked her head at him, implying yet another question.

''He was bothering a lady,'' Slocum said.

''I see,'' said Demmi. She sipped some wine. Charlie had at last finished his first glass of whiskey, and he poured himself another.

''And so the rest of his family came after you,'' Demmi said. ''God. What then?''

''Not much,'' Slocum said. ''They jumped us twice, and me and that little detective killed all but two of them. Them last two said that it was all over. They wouldn't try no more.''

"Did you believe them?'' she asked.

"Yeah,'' said Slocum. "Sure.''

"The police captain said that you'd been attacked on the train,'' Charlie said. "And he implied that there might be a connection to what happened here.''

"That was later,'' Slocum said.

"And it was not the family that had been after you?''

Slocum shook his head.

"No,'' he said. "This one was different altogether.''

"I see,'' said Charlie. "Well, I hope it all gets straightened out soon. I had to take time off from my job to be here.''

"What's your line of work?'' Slocum asked.

"I'm a bank teller,'' said Charlie. "That's pretty dull compared to your life.''

"It sounds sensible to me,'' Slocum said. "Hell, I'm alone most of the time out in the middle of nowhere, and I'm mostly broke, too. Don't let our cousin here fool you with all that talk about how exciting my life is.''

11

The policeman Cofy had left behind walked into the bar and strode over to the table where the three cousins were sitting. He tipped his hat to Demmi.

"Everything seems to be all right here," he said.

"Pretty quiet, Officer," said Charlie.

"Have the others all gone to their rooms, Officer—"

"O'Hara, ma'am," said the policeman. "Yes, they have. Well, all but two. Two gentlemen. I guess they're all right. Two of them together. They were on their way up to the rooms when I last saw them. I just thought I'd check on you three."

"I think I'll turn in myself," said Charlie.

"I think perhaps we all should," said Demmi. "It's late. I'd have been long asleep if it hadn't been for that awful business."

Slocum finished his drink and stood up. "We'll all go to our rooms and let you off the hook," he said.

"Oh, don't worry about me," O'Hara said. "I'll be up and watching all night. I have my orders."

In the hallway just at the top of the stairs, Sten Comlo leaned with one hand on the railing. He was looking at his cousin Spig Bowlig and snarling.

"I saw the way you were whispering in Romp's ear,"

he said. "What kind of secrets do you and Romp have? What are you keeping from the rest of us?"

"If I'm keeping any secrets," Bowlig said, "it's none of your affair."

"Could it be that the two of you are the killers?" Comlo asked. "Are you trying to set up just a two-way split of the inheritance? Is that it?"

"You're a fool," said Bowlig. "What's worse, you're a cowardly fool. A chicken shit. Yes. That's it. You're a little chicken shit."

"Oh, yeah?" Comlo said, backing away a few steps. "We'll see about that. We'll see how you talk when I've told that police captain about you. About you and Romp. No. I have a better idea. I'll tell our cowboy killer cousin, and we'll see how you deal with him."

"I'm not afraid of that cowboy," said Bowlig, "and I'm not afraid of you. Do whatever you like. I'm going to bed."

By this time Charlie Slocum was halfway up the stairs. As Bowlig headed toward his room, Comlo caught sight of Charlie.

"How much of that did you hear?" Comlo asked.

"Not much," Charlie said.

"Enough to tell that we were arguing, I bet," Comlo said.

"Well, yes," said Charlie. "I suppose so, but it's none of my business. I'm off to bed."

Comlo grabbed Charlie's shoulder, spinning him around. "No. Wait a minute," he said. "Someone else needs to know. In case he kills me."

"What?"

"He'll try to kill me because I know that he's the one."

"What do you mean?" said Charlie. "Talk straight."

"Cousin Bowlig is the killer, and I've found him out,"

Comlo babbled. "He'll try to kill me to shut me up. Someone else has to know about it."

"Wait a minute," said Charlie. "Calm down. Now. Just how did you find him out? How do you know he's the killer?"

"I saw him conspiring with Cousin Romp," Comlo said.

"Romp?" said Charlie. "That's—"

"Romp Casro. They were whispering with each other and looking at me. I think they picked me to be the next victim. The two of them are in it together."

"You saw them whispering?" Charlie said. "That's all? They could have been whispering about anything. Go to bed and get some sleep. This business tonight just has you upset. That's all."

"When they find me dead in the morning, you'll see that I was telling the truth," Comlo said, and he turned and almost ran down the hall toward his room. Just then, Slocum and Demmi reached the top of the stairs.

"What was that all about?" Slocum asked.

"When I came up," said Charlie, "I found him arguing with Spig. Spig walked away from it just as I came up, and Sten stopped me. He tried to tell me that Spig and Romp Casro are the killers, just because he saw them whispering together."

"And he accused Spig?" Demmi asked. "To his face?"

"Yes," said Charlie. "At least I suppose he did. I didn't actually hear that."

"Everybody will be accusing everybody else before this thing is over with," Slocum said.

"I suppose so," said Charlie. "Well, good night."

"Good night," said Demmi, and Slocum touched the brim of his hat. Out of the corner of his eye, he saw O'Hara at the bottom of the stairs.

"Everything all right up there?" O'Hara called out.

"Everything's quiet," said Slocum. "Now."

Demmi was watching Charlie, and when she saw that he had gone into his room and there was no one else in the hallway, she pulled at Slocum's arm.

"No one's looking," she said. "Let's go in your room. Quickly."

"Now, what do you mean by that?" O'Hara said, and he started up the stairs.

Slocum handed Demmi the key to his room. "Go on," he said. "I'll be right along."

Demmi hurried to Slocum's room as O'Hara mounted the stairs. As she shut the door behind her, the policeman reached the landing. He was puffing.

"Now," he said. "Just what did you mean by that comment?"

"I said everything's quiet," said Slocum. "That's all."

"You said, 'Everything's quiet—now,' " O'Hara said. "And I believe that you meant something by the way you said it."

"Well," Slocum said. "There was an argument up here between two of the heirs. That's all. Nothing to worry about. There'll be others."

"What was it about?" asked the policeman.

"One was accusing the other of being the killer," Slocum said. "Hell, I've been accused. Like I said, it's nothing to worry about. They've both gone to bed. Before this is over, everyone'll accuse everyone else."

"Who were they?" O'Hara asked.

"I don't want to point no fingers," said Slocum. "There wasn't no basis for his accusation. He seen two of them whispering. That's all."

"I still need to know," O'Hara insisted. "If something was to happen, and the captain found out about this, and I was ignorant of the facts, he'd skin me alive. So who was having an argument and who was accusing who?''

Slocum thought for a moment, scratching his head. He guessed that the policeman was right, at least from his own point of view.

"All right," he said. "It was Comlo and Bowlig arguing up here. Charlie Slocum heard them. Then Bowlig went running on to bed, and Comlo told Charlie all about it. He said that Bowlig and Casro were partners in the killing. Said he'd seen them conspiring together and looking at him. That's all."

While Slocum talked, O'Hara was taking notes. He finished with his note taking and looked up at Slocum.

"That's it?" he said.

Slocum shrugged. "I said it was nothing," he said.

"All right," said O'Hara. He tucked the notebook back into his pocket. "Thanks, and good night."

Slocum walked down the hall and opened the door to his room. Stepping inside, he shut the door behind himself. The key was in the keyhole, so he locked the door and pulled out the key. He looked at the bed, and in the moonlight streaming through the window, he saw Demmi there with a sheet pulled up to her neck. She smiled. With the door safely locked, she let the sheet fall, and Slocum saw that she was waiting there naked in his bed.

"What took you so long?" she asked.

Slocum pulled his shirt off over his head and tossed it aside.

"That watchdog policeman wanted to know what was going on up here," he said.

"Did you tell him?"

"I told him there had been an argument," he said. "Told him it was nothing."

Demmi sat up straighter and flung the sheet back farther,

inviting Slocum in. He sat down in a chair to pull off his boots.

"After what happened," she said, "I didn't want to spend the night alone in my room."

He stood to unfasten his trousers and let them drop to the floor.

"Is that the reason you're here in my bed?" he asked.

"That's one reason," she said.

Slocum's cock was about half risen in anticipation of things to come. He walked over to the bed.

"What's the other reason?" he asked.

Demmi reached out and took hold of his cock, and it stiffened in her grip. She squeezed it hard, and it jumped and bucked.

"This," she said. "I like the way you use it."

"I like the way *you* use it," he said.

She pulled him into bed by his bucking cock, and he moved on top of her, leaning forward to press his lips against hers. He found them warm and wet and open, inviting him to probe her mouth with his tongue. He thrust his tongue into her mouthh, and she sucked hard, trying to pull more of it in, trying to suck it right out of his mouth.

At the same time she spread her legs farther apart and lifted her knees. With both hands, she guided the head of his cock to just the right spot and pulled. Slocum responded by thrusting down and forward, sliding between the silky walls of her love tunnel, driving in deep, until his pelvis was pressed hard against hers, until the whole length of his cock was inside her. Then he held still, savoring the sensation.

And then she began a wonderful, pulsating, rhythmic squeezing of his cock with the muscles of her marvelous cunt. Her hands slid down his back until she had one on each cheek of his ass. First she squeezed his cheeks, and then she dug sharp fingernails in. He flinched, and her muscles milked his cock. He pulled his face away from hers, just a little, and he moaned.

"Ah, Demmi," he said. "That's good. That's real good."

Then she humped upward, grinding her flesh against his, but he was already in as far as he could go, so he raised himself, pulling his cock about halfway out, then pushing slowly in again.

"Oh. Yes," she said. "Yes, John. Screw me. Screw me good."

He pulled out again, this time almost all the way. Only the head of his cock remained in her hole, and just before it would have slipped out, he drove in deep again. Then again and again and again.

The rhythm of her upward trusts matched those of his downward drives, and she moaned out loud in her pleasure with each stroke.

"Oh. Oh. Oh."

As he slowly increased the speed of his thrusts, she kept with him, and they moved as if they were perfectly matched machines. At last they were pounding furiously into each other, each desperate plunge ending with a splat.

"Ah. Ah. Ah," Demmi moaned.

Slocum felt the pressure building and knew that surge was almost about to come. He drove hard a few more thrusts, then deep inside her, held, and she felt the first spurt, and then another and another, and she squeezed him tight around his waist with her legs, and she squeezed him with her arms, and she squeezed him with the walls of her cunt.

"Ah," she said, "I'm flooded. You filled me up, and I'm running over."

They held each other close, but slowly they relaxed, until he was lying heavily on top of her.

"Just stay where you are for a while," she said. "I like to feel you on top of me, and I like to feel you inside me."

"I ain't going nowhere," Slocum said, and he kissed her lips tenderly.

"That was wonderful," she said.

"Yeah," he said. "It was pretty damn good, wasn't it?"

His cock had softened inside her, and he backed slowly off, letting it slip free. Then he rolled over to lie beside her. Both of them were still breathing deeply.

"John," she said.

"Yes?"

"I don't know what we're going to get out of Uncle Ferdie—if anything—but whatever it turns out to be, this is going to be the best thing about this entire episode."

"You know what?" he said.

"What?"

"You and me feel just exactly the same about that."

12

Breakfast with the heirs didn't take place the next morning the way it had before. They were up and about at different times, their rest having been severely disturbed the night before. Demmi had slipped out of Slocum's room and back into her own to freshen up and change clothes for the day, and a little later they met as if by chance in the hotel lobby.

"Have you had your breakfast, Mr. Slocum?". Demmi asked, a coy expression on her face.

"Why, no, ma'am," said Slocum. "Would you care to join me?"

"I'd be delighted," she said, and they walked together into the dining room. They were met just inside the door by a host who escorted them to a table and presented them with menus. Slocum noticed that Comlo and Bowlig were sitting at separate tables and periodically glaring at each other. Nerlcut and Casro were sitting together, and Lawyer Lewes was seated with Marty Bloe and Charlie Slocum. Within a minute after Slocum and Demmi were seated, Nerlcut and Casro, their meal done, got up to leave.

A waiter came to the table, and Slocum and Demmi placed their orders for breakfast and coffee. The coffee was served quickly. It was hot and fresh. Demmi took a tentative sip from her cup.

"Um, good," she said.

"If I was a gentleman," said Slocum, "I'd say that this meal is on me, but it's all on that lawyer fellow anyhow, so—what the hell?"

"Exactly," Demmi said. "What the hell?"

Their breakfast was served, and while they were eating, Comlo stood up to leave. On his way out he passed close by Bowlig's place, slowed down, and glared into the other man's face.

"I wish you'd quit staring at me like that," he said, and he stalked on out of the dining room.

"I'm afraid," said Demmi, her voice low, "there's going to be trouble between those two."

Slocum took a swallow of coffee and put down his cup.

"Likely," he said.

"Do you really think that one of them might be the killer?" she asked.

He shook his head.

"I don't believe either one's got the nerve for it," he said.

They finished eating, and their dishes were cleared away in a moment. Then their coffee cups were quickly refilled.

"I don't guess I've ever felt quite so pampered," said Slocum. "Well, at least not in an eating place."

Just then Cofy walked into the room. He stopped just inside the door and looked the room over. The host approached him, but the policeman dismissed him with a wave of the arm. He spotted Slocum and Demmi and walked directly to their table.

"Mind if I join you?" he asked, but not waiting for an answer, he pulled up a chair.

"Reckon not," said Slocum.

A waiter was at his side by the time he was sitting.

"Bring me a cup of black coffee," Cofy said. As the waiter hustled away for the coffee, the policeman turned toward Slocum. "I heard there was a bit of a commotion here last night," he said.

"No more'n that," said Slocum, and he recounted the details of the encounter between Comlo and Bowlig for the captain. "That's all there was to it," he added.

The waiter returned and placed a cup of steaming hot liquid in front of the policeman, who picked up the cup immediately and took a long and loud slurp.

"I wish your dear departed uncle had picked another city for this gathering," he said.

"Yeah," said Slocum. "I expect you do."

About then Bowlig got up to leave the room, and Cofy watched him until he was out the door.

"That one of them?" he asked.

"Yup," said Slocum.

"That's Cousin Spig Bowlig," said Demmi.

"Bowlig," Cofy muttered, and he took another slurp from his cup. "Where's the other one?"

"Comlo?" Slocum asked.

"He left a few minutes ago," said Demmi. "I suppose he went back to his room. I don't know."

Suddenly they heard a shout from the lobby.

"Sten. What the hell are you doing with that? Don't. Don't. You crazy—"

Two shots rang out, followed by shouts and screams. Cofy jumped to his feet, upsetting the cup in front of him. He ran toward the door that led to the lobby, and Slocum was not far behind him. Out in the lobby, they saw the bleeding body of Spig Bowlig at the foot of the stairs. About halfway up the stairs stood Sten Comlo, a small pocket pistol in his hand. Cofy and Slocum both pulled out their revolvers. Comlo backed up the stairs a few steps.

"Comlo!" shouted Cofy. "This is the chief of police. Stop where you are and put down that gun."

"No," said Comlo. He backed up a few more steps.

"Put it down," Cofy said. "And stand still."

"I can't," said Comlo. "It wasn't my fault." He backed up another step.

"Put down the gun, and we'll talk about it," said the policeman.

"He was going to kill me," said Comlo, backing up some more. "I shot him in self-defense."

"Maybe so," said Cofy. "Put down the gun and then you can tell me all about it."

"You'll put me in jail," Comlo said. He backed up some more, and he had nearly reached the top step. "I don't want to go to jail. It wasn't my fault. It wouldn't be fair to put me in jail."

"Comlo," said Cofy, "for the last time, stand still and put down the gun. I don't want to have to shoot you."

Comlo looked nervously over the hotel lobby below him. Cofy and Slocum both held guns on him..Cofy was a chief of police and Slocum a western gunfighter. Comlo knew that he didn't have a chance if he tried to shoot it out with them. He didn't wat to be shot to death, but he was terribly afraid of going to jail or of being executed for murder. It seemed all of a sudden as if the lobby below was filled with the curious, all staring at him, all waiting to see what would happen, all watching to see him shot full of holes. He couldn't stand it.

"All right," he said. "All right. Don't shoot."

"No one's going to shoot, if you put down the gun," Cofy said.

Comlo leaned forward slowly, reaching toward the step he stood on with his gunhand.

"I'm putting it down," he said. "Don't shoot. I'm putting it down."

He bent his knees, still reaching for the step. Then he

turned quickly, diving for the floor of the landing. He was out of sight of the people down on the main floor. Cofy started running up the stairs with Slocum right behind him.

Up on the landing, Comlo raced down the long hallway as fast as he could. He reached the end of the line and looked back over his shoulder to see Cofy's head appearing as the policeman was coming to the head of the stairs. Desperately he looked around. He grabbed the nearest door handle and jerked open the door before hurrying through.

Cofy and Slocum reached the landing just in time to see the door slam shut at the far end of the hall. "Come on," Cofy said, and he ran down the hallway. Slocum caught up with him, passed him, and jerked open the door. He saw a stairway that only went up. There was no sign of Comlo, but there was no place he could have gone other than up the stairs. Slocum mounted the stairs three at a time. Cofy was hurrying behind him.

At the top of the stairs Slocum found himself facing another door. He pulled it open to discover that it led outside. He saw the sky. He was on the roof of the hotel. He stepped out cautiously and looked around, not seeing Comlo anywhere. Chimneys, smokestacks and other structures Slocum did not recognize provided all kinds of cover for the fugitive. Cofy stepped out beside Slocum.

"I don't see him," Slocum said.

"There's a ladder over there," said Cofy. "A fire escape. If he's got any brains left about him, he'll head for that. Come on."

Cofy moved slowly toward the far edge of the roof. Slocum spotted the rails which indicated where the ladder went down the side. Suddenly Comlo came out from behind a chimney and fired three shots. Slocum hit the deck. Cofy yelped and grabbed at the side of his head. Then he dropped to one knee.

"Get away. Get away!" Comlo yelled, and he ran to the edge of the roof there by the handrails. Slocum pointed his Colt.

"Stop right there," he yelled.

"I'll kill you both!" Comlo shouted, and he aimed again at Cofy, who still knelt holding the side of his head.

"Throw down the gun," Slocum called.

"No," said Comlo, and he fired again, the bullet kicking the roof just beside the stunned policeman. Slocum fired. A splotch of dark red appeared on Comlo's left shoulder. He shrieked and flung away the pistol he was holding. He staggered back, tripped, looked over his shoulder, and, horrified, screamed again. He fell back over the edge of the building, and his shriek did not stop until he hit the pavement below. Slocum ran to Cofy's side.

"How bad you hit?" he asked.

"I don't know," said Cofy. "Must not be too bad or I'd be dead. It's the side of my head. My ear."

"Let me see," said Slocum.

Cofy moved his hand away from the wound, and Slocum could see that Comlo's bullet had grazed the side of Cofy's head and torn his ear. It was a slight wound but a very bloody one.

"You're right," he said. "It looks a hell of a lot worse than it is. Your left ear ain't never going to be as pretty as the right one again though. Come on. Let's get you back inside the hotel."

He put an arm around Cofy's back and helped him to his feet.

"Where's Comlo?" Cofy asked.

"I had to shoot him," said Slocum, "and he went over the edge."

"Damn," said the police chief. "What a mess."

"Hell," said Slocum, "I didn't seem to have no choice. He was drawing a fresh bead on you."

"No, no," said Cofy. "I'm not blaming you. In fact I thank you. God, I'm dizzy."

They reached the door they had come out from and started back down the stairs. Cofy had to stop a time or two along the way, but they made it to the floor with the rooms, down the hallway to the landing, and down the main stairway to the hotel lobby. Slocum led Cofy to a chair, then waved at the desk clerk who came running.

"Oh, my," he said. "Oh, my."

"Stop blubbering," said Slocum, "and get a doc over here to take care of the chief."

"Yes," the clerk said. "Right away."

He ran off again, and Demmi came over to Slocum and Cofy.

"Is O'Hara here?" Slocum asked.

"That other policeman is here," she said. "Someone came running in and said that a man had fallen off the roof. He went outside."

"Good," said Cofy. "I need a man out there."

"Are you hurt badly?" Demmi asked.

"He'll be all right," said Slocum. "And that was Comlo who went off the roof."

"Oh, my God," said Demmi.

Kirt Nerlcut stepped up just then, followed close by Romp Casro. Nerlcut looked over his shoulder and spoke low to Casro.

"Spig and Sten are both dead now," he said. "That's three of us gone."

Lawyer Lewes came running up to join the little group.

"God, what next?" he asked, not really expecting anyone to answer him.

"Mr. Lewes," said Cofy. "Just as soon as I get cleaned

up, I want to talk to your group again. Would you get them all together?''

"What's left of us," said Casro.

"Yes," said Lewes. "Of course."

The doctor arrived and pushed his way through the crowd. As they separated, Casro looked at Slocum.

"Another notch on your six-shooter?" he said.

"I don't carve notches on my guns, Rump," Slocum said, "but if I ever decide to do you in, I'll carve my first one just for you. I promise you that—cousin.''

13

Lewes gathered the remaining heirs together in a small banquet room just off the main dining room. In another few minutes a patched-up Cofy came into the room.

"Chief Cofy," said Lewes, "are you all right?"

"Yeah," said the chief. "I'm okay. I'll be a damn sight better, though, when you and your crew have cleared out of here."

"What's the matter, Chief?" asked Nerlcut. "The killer's dead now, isn't he?"

"Now, just who do you mean?" asked Cofy.

Nerlcut looked around at the others, as if seeking support.

"Well," he said. "Cousin Sten Comlo, of course. We all saw him shoot Cousin Spig. There's no doubt about it."

"No," said Romp Casro. "Sten wasn't the killer. He was just terrified of Spig. He said Spig was the killer and was planning to kill him."

"Well," said Nerlcut, "either way, it's over. Right?"

With that last query he looked at Cofy.

"All of you be quiet," said the chief. "We don't know if it's over. Maybe Comlo just suspected Bowlig. Maybe the reasons for his suspicion weren't any good. We don't know if either one of those two guys was the one we're after."

"You mean the real killer may still be loose?" Marty Bloe asked.

"We just don't know," said Cofy.

"Well," said Casro, "it couldn't possibly be any of us except for Cousin John Slocum there. The killer from the West. He just killed Cousin Sten, didn't he? We know that for sure."

"That's enough of that," said Cofy. "Slocum here shot Comlo while Comlo was shooting at me. I owe him thanks for that."

"But if he's the killer," Casro continued, "he might just have taken advantage of that fight between Sten and Spig. They just played right into his hands."

"I said that's enough," Cofy said, raising his voice. He was working hard to maintain his composure with these people. He thought they were all crazy—all except Slocum anyhow. His mind raced with possibilities, and it occurred to him that there might not really be a killer. Maybe Slocum had been attacked on the train by a common thief. Maybe someone had just had a fight with Kolp, the way Comlo and Bowlig had fought. Maybe this whole notion of a plan to get rid of heirs was totally wild and untrue. Maybe.

"Lewes?" he said.

"Yes?"

"Any word on the last of your group? The one you been waiting for?"

"Sarl Diglo?" said Lewes. "No. Nothing yet. He should be getting here any time, though."

"Say," said Casro. "That's right. What about Sarl?"

"What do you mean, what about him?" Cofy asked.

"Why is he so late? Maybe he's already been murdered."

"Or maybe," said Nerlcut, "he's the murderer. After all, no one has seen anything of him. He could be hiding anywhere and slipping in to do his dirty work. When we're all dead, he'll show up and claim all the inheritance.''

Cofy didn't say anything, but he had to admit to himself that Nerlcut's latest theory had some merit. If Diglo were the killer, he might be waiting until all the others were dead, killed either by himself or by some accomplice, before coming into the city. No one would be able to prove he had been around. Perhaps he would even be able to prove that he had been elsewhere. It could have been his accomplice, or someone he hired, or even Diglo himself who had attacked Slocum on the train. It sounded good, but, of course, it was only a theory, and there was no way to act on it. Just wait and see.

Slocum sat through all this quietly, watching and listening. He could understand the killings and attempted killings motivated by greed. He had seen plenty of that before. He could understand the policeman's frustration. He was feeling some of that himself. He could even understand the suspicions and accusations, the heirs pointing fingers at one another. The thing that amazed Slocum, the thing he kept finding the hardest to believe, was that he was actually related to these people. Hell. He told himself, a man don't get a chance to choose his own family. Sure don't need to like them. Don't even need to claim them.

He began to think for the first time in his life that perhaps he had made the right choice when he had become a lone wolf, a wandering stranger among strangers. But as soon as the thought struck him, he admitted that it had not been a real choice. He had never made such a decision. Things had just worked out that way. That's all. Well, hell, he said to himself, sometimes things do work out for the best.

The rest of the day was uneventful, though nervous and tense for most of the people involved. That night Slocum again rolled in Demmi's arms. They made love once, quietly, and then they slept. Early in the morning, as usual, Demmi slipped out of Slocum's room and back into her own. They met in the morning casually for breakfast.

They had finished their meal and were drinking another cup of coffee when Lewes came walking over to their table, a worried look on his face.

"Have either of you seen aything of Kirt this morning?" he asked.

"No," said Demmi. "I haven't."

"Not me," Slocum said. "He's likely sleeping late."

"I knocked on his door and got no answer," said Lewes. "Under the circumstances, that worries me."

He hurried off without waiting for any further comment from Slocum or Demmi. A troubled wrinkle spread over Demmi's brow.

"Do you think something's happened to him?" she asked.

Slocum shrugged.

"I don't know," he said.

Demmi shoved back her chair and stood abruptly.

"Well," she said, "I can't just sit here."

She hurried after Lewes, and Slocum took another sip of the coffee. Then he looked after her, put down the cup, said, "Damn," and stood up to follow. Out in the lobby he saw Lewes talking to O'Hara. He walked over to join them. Demmi was already there.

"I'll get a key to his room," O'Hara was saying as Slocum drew close enough to hear, and the policeman hurried over to the desk. He returned to the small group in a short while with a room key in his hand. "Let's go," he said.

They crossed the lobby, climbed the stairs, and walked about halfway down the hallway to Nerlcut's room. O'Hara knocked. There was no response from inside the room. He knocked again. Still nothing.

"Mr. Nerlcut," he called. "Mr. Nerlcut. Are you in there?" He knocked again, louder than before.

Demmi stepped forward, practically pushing her face against the door.

"Kirt!" she shouted. "Kirt. It's Demmi. Open the door if you're in there. Wake up, Kirt."

O'Hara looked at Lewes, and Lewes nodded toward the door. O'Hara put a hand on Demmi's shoulder and gently pushed her to one side. He stepped up to the door and put the key in the lock. He turned the key and tried the knob. The door opened. He hesitated. Everyone wondered what they would find in Nirlcut's room.

O'Hara shoved the door wide open and stepped inside. Lewes and Demmi followed quickly. Slocum waited and stepped in last. There was no sign of Kirt Nirlcut. The bed was made. Nirlcut's clothes and other belonging were still in the room, but he was not there.

"Where could he be?" Demmi said.

"He could be anywhere," Slocum said. "Maybe he got sick of this place and went out for a while, just to get away from it."

"Maybe," said Lewes.

"Chief Cofy said that no one should go out alone," said O'Hara. "If he went out, he went alone. All the rest of you are here in the hotel."

"I've looked everywhere in the hotel," said Lewes. "I mean, everywhere that he might be within reason. I checked the dining room, the lobby, even the bar, and now we've checked his room."

"Maybe he'll show up soon," Demmi said, but her voice did not have a tone of strong conviction.

They went back out into the hall, and O'Hara relocked the door.

"I'll get ahold of the chief," O'Hara said. "I expect he'll want us to conduct our own search. Just you leave it to us, Mr. Lewes."

Cofy showed up with a squad of policemen. They started on the roof, and they searched every room in the hotel. In the lobby they looked everywhere, behind every counter and every door. They checked all closets. They looked again in the dining room and bar, and they even checked in the kitchen.

The squad had gathered around Cofy again in the lobby. The chief was scratching his head and frowning.

"There's nothing left but the basement," he said. "If we don't find him there, we'll fan out from the hotel and start searching the city. Go on downstairs, boys."

The policemen headed for the basement, and Cofy followed them slowly, looking like a man who would much rather have been at home in bed. Lewes and the remaining heirs—all except Slocum—were huddled up in the lobby watching and waiting anxiously for any news. As early as it was, Slocum had gone to the bar for a drink of whiskey.

The policeman in the lead was about halfway down the stairs when he heard a horrible shriek. It startled him, but he recovered himself quickly and looked down into the basement to see a hotel maid in hysterics running toward him. Racing up the stairs, she ran into his arms. He held her tight and shook her a little.

"Here, here," he said. "Get hold of yourself. What is it?"

"Down there," she said. "Down there."

"Where? What is it?"

"In the basket," she said.

"Laundry basket, Sarge," said the policeman next in line.

"Take care of her," said the first policeman, and he moved around the maid on down the stairs. A few feet away was a large canvas bag stretched on a metal frame on rollers. It was filled with soiled linen. He hurried over to the laundry bag and looked inside. He stood staring as the rest of the squad, save the one with the maid, crowded around him. No one spoke.

"Move aside," said Cofy, and he shoved his way through the policemen up to the edge of the basket. "God damn it," he said. Looking down into the pile of soiled linen, he saw the body of Kirt Nerlcut. The throat had been slit from ear to ear. All in all, it was a bloody mess.

14

The group of heirs to the unspecified estate of Ferdinand Slocum had dwindled to six: Romp Casro, Marty Bloe, Charlie Slocum, Demmi Bloe, John Slocum, and the yet to appear Sarl Diglo. Those who had relaxed with the killings of Comlo and Bowlig were in a renewed state of panic with the death of Nirlcut. Obviously neither Comlo nor Bowlig had been the killer, since Nirlcut's death had occurred after theirs.

And there was no longer any doubt in anyone's mind that the killings were the result of someone's effort to rid the world of heirs to Uncle Ferdie. The only suspects were therefore the heirs themselves. Slocum didn't know what Chief Cofy was thinking, but he himself had narrowed down the list to one: the absent Diglo.

Diglo was Slocum's number-one suspect for one reason only. He had been selected by the process of elimination. Slocum did not believe any of the others to be capable of the killings. Not that he didn't think them capable of murder. He just didn't think that any of them were capable of having committed these particular murders.

Romp Casro, whom Slocum insisted on calling "Rump," was a blustering bully, all talk and no action. Marty Bloe was a bit of a sissy. If Demmi was a killer, she wouldn't be the kind to have a fight with a man trying to strangle him. Charlie Slocum was a bank teller and a pretty nice guy. He'd have to be driven to kill someone. He wouldn't plan a string of murders for profit. That left only Diglo.

Slocum knew nothing about Diglo. He had never seen the man in his life as far as he knew. But it could be no one else. And, of course, there was Diglo's mysterious absence. Someone had already suggested that Diglo's tardiness might be a ploy to cover up his guilt. He could be planning to arrive late, after everyone else had been killed, and claim that he had only just arrived. In reality he might be lurking about the city. Might have been there all along.

The man who had attacked Slocum on the train might have been hired by Diglo. For that matter, Diglo could have hired more than one man. He might really still be out of town, and his hirelings might be doing the dirty work. Or it might have been Diglo himself that Slocum and Blenstool threw off the train. Perhaps he had not really been hurt by the fall. He might have survived it and come along on another train.

Whatever the case, Slocum was convinced that Diglo was the man, and he was anxious for Diglo to show himself. He wondered if Diglo would actually eliminate all of the other heirs before making his appearance. That would seem to be too obvious. It would make more sense to leave one or two others. That way he wouldn't be the only living suspect.

Slocum had lunch with Demmi, and they talked about some of the things he had been thinking about all morning. He was starting to get tired of the subject. At one point he told himself that he should slip out of the hotel, find his way back to the stable near the railroad tracks, pick up his 'paloose and head west.

But then Demmi and Charlie Slocum would be stuck in

St. Louis with Romp Casro, Marty Bloe, and the lawyer
forever. Lewes wouldn't read the will until all the survivors
were there together. And then he'd probably send Blenstool
out after Slocum again. The thought didn't stay long, but
it was nice while it lasted. It was about midafternoon when
Slocum told Demmi that he was going out.

"Where, John?" she asked.

"I don't know," he said. "I just need to get out of here
for a while. I'll walk the streets and see what I can see."

"But Chief Cofy said—"

"I know what he said," said Slocum, "and I don't give
a damn. I'll be back by suppertime. Okay?"

"What do I say if Cofy comes looking for you?"

"Tell him I'll see him at suppertime. Same as I just told
you."

Slocum left the hotel, turned to his left, and started walking. The street was crowded the way he remembered it from
his ride in, but he was surprised that he didn't have to
dodge people with every step. Amazingly, the crowd parted
to avoid him. At least it seemed that way to Slocum. He
had walked only about half a block when a man failed to
get out of his way. There was no way around the man, so
Slocum stopped. So did the other.

"Say, buddy," said the man, "can you spare a half a
buck? I ain't et in three days."

Slocum looked the man in the eyes. He was dressed well
enough, but he did have a ragged, pitiful look to his face.
Slocum dug into his jeans and pulled out a dollar. He put
it in the man's hands.

"Eat hearty," he said.

"Thanks, pal," said the man. Slocum stepped around
him and continued on his way. A carriage came racing
down the street, and two people, a man and a woman, had
to run to get out of its way. The driver didn't seem at all

concerned. Two old women stood right in the way of the foot traffic gossiping. They parted traffic the way Moses was supposed to have parted the Red Sea.

Slocum walked two full city blocks this way. Then he crossed one more street and went into a bar on the corner. It was dark inside, and it took a moment for Slocum's eyes to adjust. When they did, he walked over to the bar and leaned an elbow on it. Four men were sitting at the bar drinking beer from large mugs. The bartender stepped over to Slocum, swiping at the counter with a towel.

"What'll you have, Cowboy?" he asked.

"Kentucky bourbon," said Slocum.

The bartender brought a bottle and a glass and put them down in front of Slocum. He poured the first drink, and Slocum tossed it down. He reached into his pocket for some money, which he tossed down on the countertop.

"The whole bottle?" the bartender asked.

"Yeah," said Slocum. He picked up the bottle and the glass and headed for a nearby table. Two men sat at a table in the far corner nursing beers, and three men sat at another table not far from where Slocum plopped himself down. They had a bottle in the middle of the table. Slocum poured himself another drink and took a sip.

It was good whiskey, and it felt good to be away from the damned hotel and the crazy relatives. Slocum still felt cramped in the city, but just getting out of the hotel for a while was a relief. He kept himself from looking directly at any of the other customers, but he couldn't stop himself from wondering if one of them might not be Sarl Diglo, hiding out just two blocks away from the scene of his crimes.

If not Diglo himself, perhaps one or more of the men in the bar was a Diglo accomplice. Slocum realized that he was speculating wildly. He was in a city with thousands of people, all strangers to him, and he was imagining that one or two of these people were the killer or killers responsible for the mayhem among his newfound kin. If he didn't get out of this situation soon, he told himself, he'd wind up as crazy as the others back at the hotel.

He finished his second drink and pulled out a cigar and lit it. After a couple of puffs, he poured another glass of whiskey. After he had finished that one, he discovered that he was bored with his surroundings. He didn't really want to go back to the hotel, but neither did he want to sit alone in this strange bar and get drunk.

Just then the door opened and a man came in from the street. Slocum recognized him as the man he had given a dollar, the man who claimed not to have eaten for three days. Slocum watched as the man stepped up to the bar and proudly put down his dollar, calling for rum.

Slocum stood up, grabbed his bottle by the neck and walked to the bar to stand right next to the bum. He put the bottle on the bar.

"Howdy, partner," he said.

The man looked at him, and his eyes opened wide with recognition.

"I-I—"

"Ain't et in three days, huh?" Slocum said.

"Well, I—"

Slocum shoved the bottle over in front of the wretch.

"Here," he said. "It's already paid for."

He walked back out onto the street, and the light made him squint his eyes. He turned left and continued walking away from the hotel. Eventually he found himself back at the railroad tracks. He went to the stable to visit his horse, and he had to fight off an almost overwhelming impulse to saddle up and ride west. Then, realizing how far he had walked and how late it was getting, he started walking back.

He was about halfway back to the hotel, and his legs and feet were hurting. He was not used to walking long distances, especially not on city pavement. He was thinking that he had been pretty damned foolish, as he stepped past a narrow space between two buildings. The sun was already low in the sky, and the narrow path was dark.

Someone reached out from between the buildings, grabbing him by the collar and pulling into the darkness. He tried to turn and defend himself, but he was off balance, caught by surprise. Before he had time to recover, he felt himself struck across the forehead by something solid. He fell back against a brick wall.

The combination of the dim light between the buildings and the furious, surprise assault made it impossible for Slocum to get a good look at his attacker. The man was swinging a club at him, and Slocum, stunned by the first blow, was doing well to ward off the fast swipes with his forearms.

Unable to pound in Slocum's head, the man suddenly changed his tactics, dropped the club, and, growling like a wild animal, lunged with both hands at Slocum's throat. Slocum reached for the strangling hands with his own, trying to pry them loose from his throat.

He was gasping for breath. There was no doubt about it. The man was trying to kill him. Slocum pulled at the fingers, but he could not loosen the man's grip. He knew that if he didn't do something fast, he would be dead. He felt himself weakening fast, and he asked himself, where was the man the most vulnerable, and how easy would it be for him to take advantage of that vulnerability?

He was not quite in a position to drive a knee into the man's groin. What else? What else? The eyes? He couldn't bring himself to turn loose of the hands. If nothing else, his prying at the fingers was taking some of the pressure off his throat. Then it came to him.

He put all his weight on his left foot and felt around with his right foot. He found the man's foot, raised his own and brought the heel of his boot down as hard as he could across the top of the shoe, just about where the laces would be tied. The man screamed in pain and released his death grip on Slocum's throat.

Slocum sank back against the wall gasping for breath. He wanted to take advantage of the moment, but he couldn't seem to move. The wounded man roared in pain and anger and swung a large fist at the side of Slocum's head, and Slocum just had the foresight and energy to roll with the punch. Even so it was a stunning one.

Then the man started driving his fists into Slocum's midsection, a right and a left, one after the other. Slocum tightened his stomach and took the punches, all the while sizing up the new situation. The big man thought that he had Slocum where he wanted him. He wasn't worrying about his own guard.

Slocum waited for just the right opportunity, then put all his strength into a vicious right-hand uppercut. He caught the man square under the chin. The man straightened up, stood still for a moment, then staggered back a couple of steps. When he put his weight on his injured foot, he staggered to one side.

Slocum moved quickly then, swinging his right leg, catching the man just under the knees and knocking his legs out from under him. The big man landed hard on his left side. Slocum dropped down on top of the man's chest, intending to pound his face into mush, but the man grabbed a handful of Slocum's hair and jerked him forward. Slocum did an involuntary somersault, landing in a sitting position back out on the sidewalk.

He shook his head, trying to clear it, turned onto his hands and knees and stood up on unsteady feet. Then he lunged back into the dark and narrow passageway between the two buildings. His attacker was running, with a decided limp, toward the back of the buildings. He was already halfway there.

For just a second or two, Slocum thought about chasing the man, but he told himself that he'd never catch him. For another second, he thought about drawing his Colt and shooting, but two things stopped him from doing that. He had never liked the idea of shooting a man in the back, even a sneak attacker like this one. And then, he wasn't at all sure how Chief Cofy would take the news of his shooting a stranger in the back. About the worst thing he could think of was jail in the big city. He stood there until he could no longer see the man.

If I see him again, though, he told himself, I'll know him. I'll know a big man with a serious limp from some broken bones in his left foot. He knew that he had broken some of the tiny foot bones when he had stomped the man with his bootheel. So the big man would not only have a limp, it would be a fresh and painful limp from recent breaks. The foot would be sore and tender. There might even be swelling. It might not fit back into the shoe. I'll know the son of a bitch, he said to himself. I'll know him.

15

It was full dark by the time Slocum reached the hotel, and he was just as glad for it. He figured that his face was probably a mess, bloody, bruised, and dirty, and he wasn't crazy about letting anyone see him that way. He would have to tell Cofy about the fight, of course, but he didn't really want to deal with that just yet, either. He just wanted to clean up and get some rest. That's all. The other stuff could wait awhile. Morning would be plenty soon to tell Cofy.

But the hotel lobby would be full of people and well lit. There was no way he would get through there unseen. He walked around the corner of the building and made his way to the back. A stairway with a landing at each floor went up the back side of the building. Slocum looked around. He saw no one, and so he mounted the stairs. His bones and muscles ached with each step. Reaching his floor, he tried the door but found it locked.

"Shit," he said.

He reached down into his pocket and pulled out a folding knife. Opening a blade, he pried at the lock, and soon it clicked free. Slocum turned the knob on the door and opened it just a slit. He peeked into the hallway. A hotel guest he did not know was just opening a door to a room.

No one else was in the hallway, and the unknown guest did not appear to have noticed Slocum.

Slocum waited until the man had gone into his room, then slipped quickly into the hallway and hurried on down to his own room. He unlocked the door and went inside, then locked it again behind himself. He hung his hat on a peg on the wall, pulled his shirt off, and tossed it aside, then stepped up to the mirror on the wall to take a look at himself.

"Damn," he said. He was glad he had not gone through the lobby. He slopped some water out of the pitcher into the bowl that stood beside it on the small table there beneath the mirror. Leaning over the bowl, he washed his face, then dried it with the towel. He walked over to the bed and sat on the edge to pull off his boots. Then he heard a light rapping at his door. He jerked out his six-gun and stepped quickly across the room to the door.

"Who is it?" he said.

"It's Demmi," came the answer. "Open up. Hurry."

Slocum holstered his revolver, unlocked and opened the door, and Demmi slipped quickly into the room. She looked at his cut and bruised face with wide eyes.

"God," she said, "what happened to you?"

"Hell," he said, "a fellow jumped me out on the street. He got away, but he ain't in much better shape than I am."

"Who was it?" Demmi asked.

"I don't know," he said, "but if I see him again, I'll know him. At least, I think I will."

"The others have been asking about you," she said. "When you didn't show up for supper, we got worried."

"Well, I meant to be back, but then I wasn't expecting no tussle. That slowed me up some."

"I'd better go tell them you're here," she said, "and that you're all right. Well, sort of."

Slocum put a hand on her shoulder.

"Wait a minute," he said. "Do you know Cousin Sarl Diglo?"

"Not well," she said. "I haven't seen him since we were children. Why?"

"Never mind," he said.

"You think he did this?"

"I don't know," said Slocum. "Is Cofy downstairs?"

"Yes. He is."

"Well, go on down then, and tell them to quit worrying," he said, "and if you don't mind, ask the clerk to send me up a hot bath."

She stood and looked him up and down.

"I'll do that," she said. "You need it." She started to leave the room, then paused, looking back over her shoulder. "Oh," she said, "when they bring it—don't lock your door. I'll be back."

Slocum smiled. Ordinarily, and especially with what was going on around him, he wouldn't think of getting naked and down in a tub of hot water with his door unlocked. But this was something else.

"Don't be too long," he said.

Demmi went to the desk and ordered Slocum a bath. She was going to go back up to her room when Chief Cofy stopped her.

"Have you seen anything of Slocum yet?" he asked.

She looked around to make sure no one else was close enough to hear what she had to say. Then she leaned in close to Cofy and spoke low.

"As a matter of fact," she said, "I just left him. He's in his room."

Cofy started to move toward the stairs, but Demmi stopped him with a hand on his arm.

"Don't go up just now," she said. "He's ordered a bath.

I'm sure he'll tell you all about it soon enough."

"All about what?" Cofy asked.

"He's had a fight, and he's pretty beat up," said Demmi. "That's why he ordered the bath. Give him time to get cleaned up and rested. Will you?"

"Well, maybe," said Cofy. "What do you know about this fight?"

"Not much," Demmi said. "He was walking down the street, and someone jumped him. He didn't recognize the man. He was big. That's all he said. He'll tell you all about it later. Okay?"

Cofy scowled and hesitated.

"All right, Chief?" Demmi said, her voice insistent.

"All right," said Cofy. "I guess it'll wait—but not for long."

"Won't the morning be soon enough? I promise you, he can't tell you much more than he told me, and I've already told it to you. He's here, and he's all right. Let him get a good night's sleep."

"All right," said Cofy. "First thing in the morning."

"Thank you," she said, and she went into the bar where she ordered herself a drink. She carried the drink back into the lobby, found a comfortable place, and sat down. She watched until she knew that Slocum's bath had been provided. Then she waited only a few more minutes before climbing the stairs, first making sure that she was not being watched. She made her way to Slocum's room and slipped in, shutting and locking the door behind herself. She turned and looked at Slocum.

He was sitting in the tub, his revolver in his hand. When he saw that it was Demmi coming into his room, he laid the gun aside. She walked slowly and seductively toward him, a half smile on her face.

"Feeling any better?" she asked.

"A little," he said.

She knelt beside the tub and reached for the sponge that was floating on top of the sudsy water. Then carefully and gently she bathed his face, washing away the dirt and the crusted blood. Then she kissed him on the lips and, reaching around, began to scrub his back with the sponge.

"Um," she said, "this is awkward. I'll get my dress all wet."

"I'd hate for you to get your dress all wet," said Slocum.

"I know how to deal with this situation," she said, and she stood up to undress. Slocum watched her eagerly as she peeled off her clothes, slowly revealing more and more of her lovely body. As soon as she had stripped off the last item, she stepped over the edge and into the tub.

"I'm glad they brought a nice big tub," she said, spreading her legs to sit astraddle of Slocum.

He put his hands on her narrow waist.

"Yeah," he said. "Me, too."

A thrill went through his body as he felt the back of her thighs and her smooth round ass settle down on his legs. He reached around her and pulled her closer to him. Playfully she pushed against his chest with both hands, holding him off.

"Wait," she said. "We have to finish your bath."

She found the sponge and, reaching around him, resumed washing his back, but in order to do so, she had to press herself against him. He saw her breasts mash against his chest, and felt her hairy crotch press against his belly. He also felt his own rod begin to rise underneath her. He knew that she would feel it, too.

She finished washing his back and eased herself away from him so she could scrub his chest, then his belly, and then she was reaching down between her own legs to wash his now stiff cock and heavy balls.

"Oh," she said. "So anxious?"

"Raring to go," he said.

"I knew you weren't hurt badly," she said.

She played with his cock for a while under pretense of washing it, then raised herself slightly and eased forward just a little. She still held his cock, and she maneuvered it into just the right position, then eased herself down on it, letting it slide comfortably into her wet and silky cunt.

"Oh," she said. "Oh, that's nice. That's very nice."

She thrust her hips forward against him, feeling the hard rod drive more deeply into her, then eased back again. Then she started to slide back and forth with a regular rhythm. Slocum flexed the muscles of his ass in concert with her movements. It was all he could do with her weight pressing him against the hard bottom of the tub. The water rippled around them in response to their actions.

Then, together, as if in response to a prearranged signal, they increased their speed, and soon the water around them roiled and splashed over the edges of the tub. Slocum pressed his arms down against the edges of the tub in order to be able to raise his ass off the tub's bottom. Their bodies slapped together with each stroke.

"Oh. Oh. Oh!" she cried.

Slocum felt the impending surge building up deep inside him, and he raised himself up, driving his cock in deep, and he held his position there. She knew what was coming, and she, too, held still, her mouth open as if in amazement. Then Slocum fired his first shot, and she felt it gush into the depths of her cunt.

"Oh, my," she said.

The second spurt came fast after, and then another and another, and with each spurt she felt his rod throb inside her.

"God," she said, "you're filling me up."

Slocum shot another load, and then he relaxed.

"You just drained me," he said.

She settled down on top of him, enjoying the feeling of his still stiff cock inside her very squishy pussy. She put her arms around his neck and leaned into him, pressing her lips against his, spreading them and slipping her tongue into his open mouth. He responded in kind, and their tongues rolled around each other, probing each other's mouths. At last they parted.

"That was a wonderful, wet fuck," she said.

His cock went soft, and she raised herself slightly, letting it slip out. She reached down to feel it, and although it was no longer hard, it was still swollen. Finding the sponge, she washed it again, then stood and swiped between her legs with the sponge. She reached for the towel that was draped across the back of a nearby chair and began drying herself. Slocum stood, and she dried him, too. Then they moved over to the bed and collapsed side by side.

"You get better every time," she said.

"You, too," he said.

"God, I'm glad I found you."

"You're the best thing I've found about this whole crazy trip to St. Looie," Slocum said. "If it hadn't been for you, I think I'd have lit out for the West some time ago."

"I'm glad you came," she said, "and I'm glad you stayed."

She rolled over onto her side and with the fingers of her left hand began playing with the hairs on his chest.

"You're not still thinking about leaving, are you?" she asked.

"No, hell," he said. "I'll stick it out to the end now."

She scooted closer to him, laying her leg over his legs, putting her head on his chest, and reaching down to fondle his cock.

"Can you get it up again?" she asked him.

"No," he said. "I'm afraid not."

"Oh," she responded, disappointment evident in her voice.

"But you probably can."

"Oh, I see."

She kissed his chest and licked his nipples. Then she slid her tongue down his belly, down to the hairs of his crotch. She still gripped his cock, and she held it up to lick its head. Then she opened her mouth wide and clamped her lips around the cock head. She held it there for a moment, lapping it with her tongue. Then she pulled it loose with a loud slurp.

She took it in again, and this time she let go with her hand so she could draw the cock farther into her mouth. Farther and farther until it must have been all the way down into her throat. She sucked and slurped and lapped with her tongue, and she felt it start to swell and harden inside her mouth.

"Ummm," she murmured.

She pulled her head back until nothing but the head was left between her lips, and then she dived down it again. She began to bounce her head up and down, screwing her face with Slocum's cock. Slocum tried to lie still, but at last he was overcome by Demmi's wonderful attention, and he began to hump her face.

Then she pulled off and once again gripped his cock hard with her hand.

"Do you want to come in my mouth?" she asked him.

"Not this time," he said. "Turn around and get up on your knees."

Demmi gave him a lecherous smile.

"Ooooh," she said.

Getting up to her knees, she turned her back on him and

gripped the iron bedstead there at the foot of the bed. She looked over her shoulder to watch him as he got to his own knees and inched up close behind her round ass. Slocum put a hand on each cheek of her butt, and she arched her back, shoving the lovely roundness at him.

"I'll do it," she said, reaching back between her legs with one hand to grip his cock again, this time to guide its head into the waiting, wet slit of her cunt. She rubbed it up and down the length of her slit, then stuck the head into her waiting hole. In place, Slocum drove forward, and Demmi gasped as she felt the hot throbbing rod rammed into her from behind.

"Oh, God," she said. "Screw me, John. Screw me hard."

He gripped her waist hard and drove into her again and again, slapping himself against her beautiful butt, ramming his cock deep into her dark, damp tunnel of love. Sweat poured from his forehead, and he knew that she, too, was covered with perspiration. He drove harder and faster, sucking in deep breaths as he screwed her.

Her pendulous breasts shook with the pounding, and her ass began to redden as from a spanking.

"Yes. Yes. Yes," she said.

He slapped against her again and again. His balls felt heavy and hard, and a tingling sensation came from every part of his body and ran through his cock. He opened his mouth.

"Ahh," he moaned.

His cock suddenly spurted into her like a fire hose, flooding her cavern until the hot, sticky juice ran out and dribbled down her thighs. He hunched a few more times, then stopped still, deep inside her, pressed hard against her ass. He waited until there were no more pulses. She worked the muscles of her vagina wall as if she were milking his cock.

At last he slipped out of her and fell back on the bed,

clearly spent for the time. She turned to sit on the bed.
Both were breathing hard.

"I hope the water's still warm," she said. "I think we
need another bath."

16

When Slocum walked into the dining room for breakfast the next morning, he found Demmi already seated at a table with Cofy. Cofy stood up when he saw Slocum come in.

"Slocum," he said. "Sit down here. Join us."

"Is that an invitation?" Slocum asked.

"Take it like that," said Cofy. "It's easier that way."

Slocum pulled out a chair and sat. He looked at Demmi. Her expression gave no hint of what had gone on the night before.

"Good morning, Mr. Slocum," she said. "Did you enjoy your bath last evening?"

"Uh, yeah," said Slocum. "I did. I needed it. Thanks for ordering it up for me."

"You're welcome. Did you get a good night's sleep?"

"Yeah."

"Good," Demmi said. "I told the chief that you'd feel much better this morning."

"You may feel better," Cofy said to Slocum, "but you sure don't look too good."

"You should have seen me last night," Slocum said, "and you ought to see the other guy."

"Yeah?" said Cofy. "Tell me about him."

A waiter came to the table, and the conversation ceased while the three gave their orders. The waiter left to turn in

125

the orders and bring back the coffee. The policeman leaned toward Slocum.

"Tell me about it," he said.

"There ain't much to tell," Slocum said. "A man jumped me, and we had a fight. Before it was over, I guess I hurt him worse than he hurt me. He took off running."

"Where did this happen?" Cofy asked.

"Oh," Slocum said, "I took a long walk. I went all the way back to the depot where I came in. Checked on my horse at the stable there. I was walking back, and I figure I was about halfway when he jumped me."

"I told you to stay here," Cofy said.

"I got tired of this place," Slocum said. "That's all."

"And you didn't recognize this man?"

"I never really got a good look at him," said Slocum, "but I don't believe I ever saw him before. He was wearing city clothes—like everyone else around here. And he was a big fellow. Bigger than me."

"Would you recognize him if you saw him again?"

"If I see a big man who's walking with a gamey left foot, I'll be real suspicious of him," Slocum said. "I stomped it real good."

"I see," said Cofy. He was obviously disappointed and a little upset. Just then the waiter returned with the coffee, and the table grew silent again until he had left.

"You have any suspicions?" asked Cofy.

"Suspicions," said Slocum. "No proof."

"He asked me," Demmi said, "if I could describe Sarl."

"Sarl Diglo," said Cofy. "The heir who hasn't showed."

"That's right," she said.

"Well," the policeman said, "can you?"

"No," she said. "I haven't seen him since we were children, but I remember him as being a very big boy."

"If he walks with a limp when he shows up," Cofy said, "we'll question him real good."

The waiter came back with the breakfasts, and they started to eat. The conversation was over for the time being. Slocum tied into his breakfast like a man who hadn't eaten for two days. A good fight always made him hungry. So did a good fuck, and he'd had both the night before. His bruised jaw did hurt him a little when he chewed, but he didn't let that slow him down.

"Well, well, what happened to you?"

Slocum glanced up to see who was talking. It was Romp Casro, looking down on him with a sneer.

"Run along, Casro," said Cofy. "We don't need a fuss here just now."

"I couldn't help noticing cousin Slocum's face," Casro said. "It's obvious he's been fighting. He's a professional killer, and I've suspected him all along. I believe that I and the others, what few of us are left, have a right to know what's been going on."

"If there's anything for you to know," Cofy said, "I'll tell you about it. After breakfast. Now get along."

Casro harrumphed as he walked away, and Slocum noticed him gather with Marty Bloe and Charlie Slocum at the door for a moment before the three of them disappeared into the lobby.

"There'll be more of that," Cofy said.

"I reckon," said Slocum, and he continued eating. The waiter stopped by to refill their coffee cups. Slocum finished his plate and called for seconds on everything. A moment later Cofy finished, and soon after so did Demmi. Then Slocum's seconds were delivered, and he tied into them just as he had the first plate.

"Do you always eat like that?" Cofy asked.

Slocum glanced up at the policeman.

"Like what?" he said.

"So much," said Cofy. "I never noticed it before. You act like you haven't had anything to eat for a week."

"He had a rough night last night," said Demmi, and she smiled as Slocum gave her a sideways look.

When Slocum had at last finished his meal, the three of them drained the last coffee from their cups and stood up to leave.

"Slocum," said Cofy, "I'm going to deal with your relatives right now. You don't have to stick around to be insulted if you don't want to. You can go on up to your room."

"Hell," said Slocum, "I'll stick around for the fun."

They walked on out into the lobby and found the others still huddled together. They were in a corner of the big lobby, where a couch and several chairs were available. Cofy headed straight for them, and Slocum followed with Demmi. Lawyer Lewes had joined Casro, Marty Bloe, and Charlie Slocum, and the four seemed to scowl at Slocum as he approached them.

"All right," Cofy said, "let's get everything out in the open here. Casro, you had something you wanted to say. Say it."

"I just wonder why you don't have Cousin John Slocum there in jail," Casro said. "That's all."

"And just what would be the charge?" Cofy asked.

"Murder, of course," said Casro.

"And what would be the evidence?" asked Cofy.

"He's an admitted killer," said Casro. "He killed one of us right up on the roof of this hotel in front of witnesses."

"That was not a murder," said Cofy. "You all know the circumstances of that killing. Besides, if he hadn't done it, I might not be standing here today."

"All right, then," said Casro. "Where was he all day yesterday? He was gone all day, and then he shows up this morning with his face like that. He's been in a fight somewhere—with someone. Was it Cousin Sarl maybe? Sarl still hasn't showed up. Maybe Slocum went out yesterday and killed him. Just like he killed the others."

"That's a lot of maybes, Mr. Casro," Cofy said, "and until you have something a little more solid than that, I want you to keep your mouth shut. Do you understand me?"

"We're all in danger here," Casro said.

"Do you understand me?" Cofy said, his voice emphatic and a bit louder. He stared hard into Casro's face. Casro blinked nervously, then looked at the floor.

"Yeah, yeah," he said.

"Does anyone else have anything to say?" Cofy demanded.

Lewes tentatively held up his hand for recognition. "Eh, are you making any progress?" he asked.

Cofy heaved a heavy and exasperated sigh. "No," he said. "We don't have a damned thing to go on."

"I have something to say," Slocum said.

"Well, go on," said Cofy.

Slocum stepped forward and looked from one face to another.

"I want to know," he said, "if all of you are thinking like Rump there."

He looked at Marty Bloe, and Bloe ducked his head. He looked at Lewes, and the lawyer stammered but said nothing intelligible. He looked at Charlie Slocum.

"It does look bad, John," said Charlie.

Slocum scowled a deep scowl.

"I didn't want to come here in the first place," he said. "I don't give a damn about Uncle Ferdie's will, and I don't give a damn about any of you. You can divide it all up among yourselves. Leave me out of it. I don't want any part of it. I'm heading west, right now.''

"You can't do that," Lewes called out in a shaking voice. "I can't even read the will unless you're here."

"Write me down dead," Slocum said. "I don't give a damn."

"I can't do that," said Lewes. "You have to be here."

"I don't have to do a damn thing," Slocum said. "And you can't stop me from leaving."

"But I can," said Cofy. "I'm sorry, Slocum, but no one leaves here until this thing is all cleared up one way or another. I don't agree with your hotheaded cousin there, but I do have to say that right now, you're all suspects. Every one of you. And right now, no one person is any more suspect than any other. You got that, Casro? You're all equal suspects, and nobody leaves town. In fact, nobody leaves the hotel again without my permission. You got that, Slocum? I'm getting real fed up with this business, and I don't need any more temper tantrums, and nobody gets pampered, and nobody gets any special favors. I'm in charge here, and you'd all better damn well understand that. Now, you can sit around and pout, cuss me quietly to each other, go to your rooms and take a nap, or go to the bar and get drunk. But no more fussing. Have all of you got that?''

17

Slocum felt like an animal in a cage. He paced the floor in his room. He went to the dining room and ate more than he really wanted. He drank coffee by the pots full. He went into the bar and had a couple of drinks, but it was really much too early in the day for that, and the way things had been going, he sure didn't want to get caught drunk and off guard.

He sat in the lobby and chatted with Demmi, but they both found that they didn't have much to say. They considered going to one of their rooms together and passing the time with pleasant romps, but they also figured that it would be too obvious during the day. At last Slocum went to his room alone to nap.

His dreams were strange. He found himself surrounded by peculiar people with unpronounceable names. They alternately chatted amiably and shouted accusations at one another. Now and then one of them or Slocum himself would stumble over a bloody corpse. At one time he found himself looking through bars from the inside of a cage.

And then Demmi was there, and she was naked and crawling over his body, licking him all over as she moved. His cock stiffened and grew and throbbed, and when he rammed it into her cunt, she was no longer Demmi at all.

She was Lady Eve from Frogtown, and Slocum gave her a passionate, deep kiss.

But then she was gone, and he was standing alone in a field surrounded by dirty men with guns, all of whom looked exactly alike. No one said anything, but he knew that they wanted to kill him. He dimly recalled having killed a man who looked just like the rest of them.

They started moving closer, and Slocum bumped into a couple of them as they walked past him, and he found himself walking down a crowded city street, dodging the fast-moving traffic of pedestrians, riders, carriages. And then he heard a banging on his door, and he sat up straight in bed. He shook his head to clear it, grabbed his gun, and stepped across the room to the door.

"Who is it?" he said.

"Cofy. Open up, Slocum."

Slocum lowered his revolver and unlatched and opened the door. Cofy was standing there with a stern look on his face. He stepped into the room and shot a glance at the gun in Slocum's hand.

"Put that thing away," he said. "Get your boots and shirt on and come with me."

"What is it?" Slocum asked.

He holstered his revolver and sat on the edge of the bed to pull on his boots. Then he stood up and put on his shirt. He picked up his gun belt to strap it on, but Cofy stopped him.

"You don't need that," he said.

Slocum hesitated only a second, looking Cofy in the eyes. He finished buckling the belt around his waist.

"I needed it once before," he said.

"Follow me," said Cofy, and he led the way out of the room and down the hall to where O'Hara was standing just outside one of the rooms. Cofy opened the door to the room and stepped aside to allow Slocum to go in. Slocum moved into the doorway and saw what Cofy had rousted him out for. Charlie Slocum was lying on the bed, fully dressed, his eyes wide open, tongue protruding from his mouth. A thin rope was knotted around his throat and pulled tight. Slocum didn't have to look closer to know that Charlie was dead.

Martin Bloe was sitting in a straight chair against the far wall, his hands clasped between his knees. His face was ashen. Cofy put a hand on Slocum's shoulder to urge him on into the room. Slocum stepped in, and Cofy followed, pulling the door closed behind them and leaving O'Hara in the hall to guard the room. Slocum gave Cofy a questioning look.

"Your cousin Bloe here," Cofy said, "says he came up here looking for Charlie Slocum to have a drink with him. Says the door was slightly opened, and he peeked in and found him like this."

"That's all?" Slocum asked.

"That's all," said Cofy. "Where have you been?"

"In my room," said Slocum. "Asleep."

"Alone?"

"Sure alone," said Slocum.

"Meaning that you have no alibi, and neither does Bloe here," Cofy said. "The only progress I've made is that I have one more victim and one less suspect."

Slocum walked over close to the bed and looked down at the body. Then he looked at Bloe sitting there trembling. He turned back toward Cofy.

"I'd say you can narrow it down more than that," he said.

"Oh? How's that?" Cofy asked.

"The way Charlie was killed," Slocum said, "I don't believe that Marty there could have done it. I don't reckon Demmi could have, either."

"That just leaves you and Casro," said Cofy.

"And Cousin Diglo," said Slocum. "Don't forget him."

"Yeah," said Cofy. "I've got men out all over the city looking for him."

"Do the others know about this?" Slocum asked.

"Not yet," said Cofy, heaving a sigh. "Let's go tell them. You, too, Bloe."

They gathered again, and once again Slocum was accused, especially by Romp Casro. As before, Chief Cofy shut him up with a threat and the statement that all of them were still under suspicion. There was speculation again about the one missing heir, Sarl Diglo. Some, like Slocum, suspected him of being the killer. Others wondered if he, too, had already been murdered and they had not yet discovered the body.

"He might have been murdered somewhere along the way," Bloe speculated. "Maybe he never reached the city. We might not ever know."

"We'll find him," said Cofy. "Don't you worry about that."

"We have to find him," said Lewes, "or we'll never be able to read the will."

Slocum thought that sounded a bit fuzzy. How could the disappearance of one heir keep a will from ever being read? He didn't think that was possible, no matter what language was in the document. If Diglo failed to show for a certain length of time, a good lawyer could get the will opened up and read. He wasn't sure how long they'd have to wait, but he was pretty damn sure that it wouldn't be forever. He decided to keep quiet, though, and keep that thought to himself, at least for a while. When Cofy finally let them loose, Slocum walked over to the desk.

"Hey, pardner," he said.

The desk clerk turned around to face him.

"Yes, sir?"

"You been here all morning?"

"I've been here since seven this morning," the clerk said.

"You seen anything of a big fellow, a stranger, walking with a limp?"

"No," the clerk said. "I haven't seen anyone like that."

Slocum hadn't expected a better answer, but he thought that he might as well ask. Still, there were other ways Diglo might have gotten into the hotel. And he could even have come in the front door when the clerk's back was turned. It didn't seem likely, though, that he'd have come in the front. If he was the guilty party, then, until he was ready to show himself, he'd be sneaking around, trying to keep himself hidden.

"Ah, to hell with it," he said under his breath, and he walked into the bar for a drink. Demmi saw him go in and followed him. She found him standing at the bar, and she walked over to stand beside him.

"Mind if I join you?" she asked.

"No," he said, "I don't mind."

He ordered whiskey for himself and wine for her. Then he walked with her to a nearby table, where they sat. The bartender came right behind them with a bottle, a carafe, and two glasses. Slocum filled both glasses, then took a drink.

"What do you think, John?" she asked.

"I think Diglo's behind it all," he said. "Hell, I know he is. There's no one else it could be."

"There's Martin," Demmi said.

"He hasn't got the guts."

"Me?"

"You're a pretty strong woman," said Slocum. "I'll

give you that. But you ain't strong enough to have strangled Charlie or had that fight with Pug. You didn't bust my face up, either."

"I might have an accomplice," she said.

Slocum looked her in the eyes for a moment in silence.

"You could have," he said.

"And there's you."

"I didn't do it," he said.

"I know that," she said. "At least I believe it."

"Yeah? Well, I don't believe that you did it, either. Even with an accomplice. That leaves me back where I started."

"Diglo?"

"Diglo."

He tilted back his head to drain his glass, and as he did, a familiar figure appeared in the doorway behind the bar. Slocum put down his glass quickly and looked, and the figure seemed to notice his look. The man disappeared quickly into the room behind the bar.

"Get Cofy," Slocum said, and he was up so fast that he knocked over his chair. He ran for the door behind the bar.

"Hey!" the bartender shouted.

Slocum ignored him, smashing into the door. He found himself in a room stacked with boxes, barrels, and bottles, and he saw the man just going out a back door that led into the alleyway. Slocum ran after him, but just as he was going through the door, the man tilted a barrel over. Slocum ran into the barrel and fell over it, landing on his face.

"God damn," he said.

He scampered to his feet, ran to the door, fumbled with the handle, opened it, and hurried out into the alley. There was no sign of the man. There was no way to tell, not even to guess, which direction he might have gone. Slocum had lost him, and that was that.

"Damn," he said out loud.

Cofy stepped up behind him.

"What's this all about?" he asked. "Miss Bloe said you chased a man through here. The big man?"

"Nope," said Slocum. "A little man. Little, but he's a hell of a fighter."

"What?"

"It was Blenstool," Slocum said. "The damned little detective. That's who it was."

"Blenstool?"

"That's right."

"What the hell was he doing here?"

"I saw him standing in the doorway," said Slocum. "When he saw me looking, he ran. I chased him out here, but he got away. That's all I know."

"Blenstool?" said Cofy once again.

"He told me he was leaving town," said Slocum. "Now he shows up sneaking around the hotel. Damn it, Cofy, I liked that little man. But this sure as hell don't look good for him."

"So you say," said Cofy.

"Now what are you talking about?" Slocum asked.

"Come on," said Cofy, and he led the way back through the storage room and into the bar. He called the bartender over. "Did you see the man standing here in the doorway?" he asked. "The man that Slocum here ran after?"

"I didn't see anyone," the bartender said. "All of a sudden this guy jumped up and ran through there. That's all I saw."

Cofy walked over to where Demmi waited, and Slocum followed.

"Did you see who he was chasing?" Cofy asked.

"No," she said. "By the time I turned around to look, the man was gone."

Cofy heaved a sigh.

"Damn it, Cofy," Slocum said. "It was Blenstool."

"I don't have anyone's word for it but yours," said the policeman. "But I'll check it out."

He turned to leave the room but stopped. He was staring hard into a far dark corner of the bar. Slocum looked after his gaze, and so did Demmi.

"Is that Bloe?" Cofy asked.

"It looks like Marty," said Demmi.

Cofy walked toward the dim figure, followed by Slocum and Demmi. In a few steps they could tell that it was indeed Martin Bloe. He was sitting alone, stiff, his head down.

"Bloe?" Cofy called.

There was no answer.

"Marty?" said Demmi.

Still Martin Bloe was silent. Cofy walked faster. Within a few feet of Bloe, he stopped. Slocum moved up beside the policeman, and then he, too, could see the knife sticking out of Martin Bloe's chest. Demmi came up beside Slocum and sucked in a sharp breath when she saw the scene clearly.

"That does it," said Cofy. "That's it. From now on, no one leaves or comes into this damned hotel without my personal permission. I'm stationing cops all around the building, and I'll keep them there until this case is wrapped up. I'll keep them there if it takes a whole damned year."

18

It was late evening when Slocum went up to Demmi's room. She had asked him earlier, promising to leave the door unlocked. The body of Charlie Slocum had been removed from his room, but O'Hara was still on duty in the hallway. There were also policemen in the lobby and at every door leading in ad out of the hotel. Slocum thought it would be a good time to rob a bank on the other side of town.

O'Hara nodded at Slocum as he walked past, and Slocum was trying to decide how to go through Demmi's door without being noticed by O'Hara. Just then he heard Demmi's voice from inside her room.

"Stop!" she screamed. "Get out!"

Slocum ran to the door and threw it open. Romp Casro looked back over his shoulder. He had Demmi by both her arms, but when he saw Slocum, he released her, turned, and swung a roundhouse right, which caught Slocum by surprise and knocked him back into O'Hara, who had followed. Slocum and O'Hara fell back into the hallway.

Slocum grabbed both sides of the doorframe to pull himself to his feet, but Casro was on him in a flash, giving him a swift kick to the side of the head. Slocum fell back again. He grabbed Casro by one leg as Casro attempted to run past him. O'Hara managed to crawl out from under Slocum and struggle back up onto his own feet.

Cofy came to the top of the stairs just as O'Hara was pulling out his gun.

"Hold it, O'Hara!" Cofy shouted. "Let them beat the hell out of each other."

O'Hara shrugged and leaned back against the wall, crossing his arms over his chest. Cofy stood with his hands on his hips, scowling at the two combatants.

On the floor Slocum jerked at Casro's leg, and Casro fell back through the open door. Staggering back, he fell onto Demmi's bed. Demmi ran back into a corner. Slocum got to his feet and ran into the room. He grabbed Casro's shirtfront, jerked him to his feet, and drove a hard right into Casro's jaw, flipping him back onto the mattress and head over heels to the floor on the other side of the bed.

Casro came up, running around the bed. Slocum was moving toward him from the other direction, and they ran together hard. Casro reached for Slocum's throat, and Slocum grabbed Casro's wrists, pulling them away. With the top of his head, he butted Casro's chin, and Casro staggered back into the wall. He shook his head as Slocum came at him again, and he swung a left hook that caught Slocum on the side of the head.

He clutched at Slocum's throat again, this time pressing him to the floor. Slocum managed to get a knee in Casro's belly and, with a mighty effort, flipped Casro over his head. Casro rolled to his feet and ran out into the hall. Slocum was up and right behind him.

Casro had just about reached the head of the stairway when Slocum caught up with him, grabbing the back of his shirt in both hands and yanking hard, spinning him around and slinging him into the wall. Casro hit hard. He stood there stunned for a second, as Slocum moved in on him again, driving a fist into his gut. Casro groaned and doubled over, but as Slocum prepared to deliver a right to the side of his head, Casro swung his own right up between Slocum's legs.

Slocum roared and dropped to his knees, clutching at his balls with both hands. Casro raised a knee hard and fast, smashing it into Slocum's face and knocking him over onto his back. He kicked Slocum in the ribs, then ran again for the stairway.

Slocum staggered to his feet, the pain still shooting through his entire body, and he lurched after Casro. By the time he reached the top of the stairs, Casro had already taken several long strides down the stairs. Slocum dived headfirst, crashing into Casro's back, and both men tumbled the rest of the way down onto the floor of the lobby.

A crowd gathered around the walls of the lobby, keeping themselves well back from the two fighting men, and the two policemen coming down from the upstairs hallway. The fighters landed several feet away from each other, and both men had a hard time getting to their feet.

Casro got up first, but he stood swaying, and Slocum stood and hit him hard with a right. Casro went down again. Slocum took a couple of staggering steps toward him, just as Casro stood swinging. His own right caught Slocum and knocked him into a chair. Slocum and the chair went over backward. He reached for the wall and pulled himself to his feet.

Casro stood weaving, waiting for Slocum to move in on him again, and Slocum did. Four long unsteady strides took him close enough for another swing. He hit Casro on the jaw, causing him to stagger back. He moved in again, and hit him again, and again Casro staggered back. Slocum swung again, and Casro fell back against the desk. As Slocum came at him still, Casro grabbed the big registry off the counter and swung it against the side of Slocum's head.

By this time the manager of the hotel had come out of his office to watch horrified as the fight raged around his place of business. When Casro flung the registry, the incensed manager turned toward Cofy where the policeman stood watching.

"Chief Cofy!" he shouted. "I demand that you stop this fight!"

Cofy sighed. He wanted to let it run its course, but there was property damage to consider at this point, and he knew that if he didn't stop it, there would be a formal complaint from the hotel. He walked forward holding up a hand.

"Slocum!" he shouted. "Casro! That's enough. Stop it now. You hear me? Stop the fight."

He was right behind Slocum. Casro wound up and swung a wide right, and Slocum ducked. Casro's fist swept the air above Slocum's head and caught Cofy on the jaw, knocking him off his feet. Slocum straightened up and drove a fist into Casro's face, knocking him through the front door and out into the street.

He followed, but when he reached the street, Casro was flat on his back. Slocum staggered toward him and fell. Both men were exhausted. Neither man tried again to get to his feet. Cofy stepped out the front door holding his jaw and looking down at the two men lying there in the street beneath him, battered, bruised and bloody. The policeman stationed at the front door gave him a questioning look.

"You just stay where you are," Cofy said. "I'll get someone else to drag those two inside."

The manager came out behind Cofy. He was spluttering and complaining. Cofy let him run himself out of breath.

"They'll pay for any damages," he said finally. "Just write out a bill and give it to me." He turned to the police guard at the door. "I don't think either one of them's going anywhere soon," he said, "but just the same, keep your eyes on them."

"Yes, sir," said the guard, and Cofy went back inside. He found four policemen in there and called them together.

"Go out there," he said, "and drag those two in and get them up to their rooms."

The four policemen went outside, and Cofy walked over to the desk. The clerk stood gaping.

"Send two baths up," Cofy said. "One to each of their rooms."

Slocum sat soaking in the tub in his room. He was barely conscious and had only a vague idea how he got back to the room and into the bath. His whole body felt banged and bruised, and his face felt puffy, swollen, and sore. The hot soapy water stung him where his flesh was scratched or cut. From somewhere far off, it seemed, he heard Demmi's voice.

"John? John, are you all right?"

He moaned out loud, trying to form words for a response.

"Yeah," he said at last. "I've been worse."

"Oh, John," she said. "Thank you for coming to my rescue. I don't know what got into Cousin Romp." Then she lowered her voice, and Slocum barely heard what she said. "He said that he knew what we'd been doing—you and me—and he—well, he wanted some of the same. That's what he said. I told him to get out, and he came at me. That's when I yelled, and then you came in."

"The son of a bitch," Slocum muttered. "I'll kill him."

"You almost did," said Demmi. " 'Course, you're not much better off than he is right now."

The door opened and Cofy walked into the room with a bottle of whiskey in his hand.

"How's he doing?" he asked.

"I'm all right," Slocum slurred.

Cofy handed him the bottle and Slocum tipped it up, taking a long drink. It burned its way down his throat, and it felt good. It revived him, at least just a little. He forced his eyes open and looked up at the policeman.

"How's the other guy?" he asked.

"I'd have to say about the same as you," Cofy said. "I'd hate to have to call it. The best I can say for you is that you fell last."

Slocum sucked in some air.

"I'll say this much," he said. "I wouldn't have believed he had it in him."

"He's a professional fighter," Demmi said. "Didn't you know?"

Slocum groaned.

"Now you tell me," he said. He tipped up the bottle again. Demmi picked up the sponge and started washing his face. He winced.

"Well," said Cofy. "I guess you'll be all right."

He left the room and stood for a moment in the hall. O'Hara was standing down toward the stairway. Cofy walked down there to join him.

"I think I'll go home," he said. "We've got this place pretty well covered now. There shouldn't be any problems, but if there are, you know how to get me."

"Yes, sir," said O'Hara. "Sir?"

Cofy looked up.

"How's Mr. Slocum?"

"Oh, he's all right," said Cofy. "He's tough as hell, that one."

"I hope he's not the guilty one," O'Hara said. "I kind of like him."

"It was a hell of a fight, wasn't it, O'Hara?" Cofy said.

"Yes, indeed, it was, Chief," said O'Hara. "A real donnybrook."

Cofy laughed.

"The other fellow," O'Hara said, "is he doing all right?"

"Ah, hell," said Cofy, "I guess I should look in on him, too. Just between you and me, I don't like him. I was hoping that Slocum would beat him bad, but then, I didn't know that the man's a professional fighter. Slocum didn't, either."

He turned and headed toward Casro's room, but he didn't hurry. He had told O'Hara the truth. He didn't like Casro a damned bit, and he hoped that Casro was suffering at least as much as was Slocum. He told himself that he would actually enjoy looking at Casro's bruises and cuts and listening to him groan with pain. After all, the man had been a pain in the ass to him for several days now.

He reached the door, took hold of the knob, and turned it. "Casro," he said, announcing his entrance. Stepping into the room and looking up, he saw Romp Casro, naked, in the tub, his head dropping down onto his chest, his arms hanging loose over the edges of the tub, the soapy water stained red with Casro's blood.

19

The next morning Demmi slipped back to her own room from Slocum's, and Slocum waited for her to get dressed and go down to breakfast. When he felt like he had given her plenty of time, he left his room. Perhaps everyone already knew what was going on between them. Still they played the game, being as discreet as possible under the rather close circumstances.

He found Demmi in the dining room, seated with Lewes, the lawyer, Chief Cofy, and another man, a man Slocum had never seen before. The man was sitting on the far side of the table, across from Slocum. Even so, Slocum could tell that he was a big man.

His shoulders were broad, and his chest was thick. He filled up the white shirt, buttoned vest, and coat that he wore. And his neck bulged out of his tight collar, fastened for the necktie that he sported. Slocum judged the man to be perhaps thirty-five years old, although his receding hairline might have made him look a little older than he really was.

Slocum walked on over to the table, and Lewes stood when he saw him coming. "Sit down and join us, Mr. Slocum," he said. Demmi half turned in her seat, nodding toward the empty chair beside her. Slocum pulled it out and sat. "Mr. John Slocum," said Lewes, speaking to the stranger. "Mr. Slocum, meet Mr. Sarl Diglo."

Slocum gave a curt nod in Diglo's direction. He had been expecting Diglo, of course, but even so, this was a surprise. So, he thought, the son of a bitch showed up after all. There's still two of us to get rid of, and now he's here, out in the open. He's got a lot of gall. I'll give him that much.

"How do you do, Cousin?" said Diglo with a big smile across his face.

"I'm all right," said Slocum.

"That in itself is quite an accomplishment around here," said Diglo, "from what I've been hearing."

"You can say that again," said the nervous Lewes.

"Oh, yes," said Demmi, with a shudder. "Yes, indeed. There's only the three of us now. I hate to think what will happen next."

A waiter showed up just then, and Slocum was glad for the interruption.

"Just coffee," he said, and to himself, he added, I'm particular about who I eat with. Demmi glanced sideways at him.

"You're not eating?" she asked.

"I ain't hungry just now," he said.

"Well, I've got a breakfast coming," she said.

"That's all right."

"You'll wait for me?"

"If you want me to."

"I do," she said.

"So, Cousin Slocum," said Diglo, "what's your line?" Slocum looked over at Diglo. "What?" he said.

"What do you do for a living?"

"Anything that's honest," Slocum said. "And now and then I slip a little."

Diglo gave a hearty laugh.

"What about you?" Slocum asked.

"Stocks and bonds," said Diglo. "Stocks and bonds."

Slocum had only a vague idea what that meant, but he wasn't curious enough to ask further. He didn't really want to talk to Diglo, unless he were to ask him where he was at the time of the various killings. A few other questions crossed his mind, too. Why was he was so late arriving? Why had he showed up just when there were only three of them left alive? When did he plan to make his next move? And, oh, yes, how was his left foot?

Slocum thought, Move against me, old buddy, and it's going to be your last move. Make a move on this lady here, and I'll hurt you first, real bad, but then I'll kill you for it later. He wanted to say all those things to Diglo, for he was absolutely convinced that Diglo was responsible for all the killings, as well as for the two unexplained attacks on Slocum. But the breakfast table in the hotel dining room just didn't seem the right place for it. He wanted to get up and leave, but Demmi had asked him to wait for her. Well, he'd wait.

"Of course," said Lewes, "we can schedule the reading of the will now. I suggest that we take care of that first thing in the morning, right after breakfast."

"Why not today?" said Diglo. "Everyone's here now. Why not in an hour or so? I would like to have a little time to rest and freshen up first."

"There's a stipulation in the will that I haven't mentioned before," Lewes said. "According to the will, we're to hold the reading the first morning after the day in which all the heirs have arrived."

Diglo shrugged his wide shoulders. "That's fine with me," he said.

Lewes looked at Demmi and Slocum, and they both agreed.

"The sooner the better," said Slocum. "I want to get out of this damn city."

"Not right away, you don't. No one leaves the hotel," said Cofy. "Not until I get this other business cleared up."

"So we have to stay here another day and another night," said Demmi. She glanced at Cofy. "Just to have the will read."

"That's correct, Miss Bloe," said Lewes.

"It sounds almost," she said, "as if Uncle Ferdie wanted to trap us all together and see if we'd kill each other off."

Diglo laughed out loud.

"You know," he said, "I wouldn't put it past the old bastard."

Slocum gave Diglo a hard look, and just then the waiter showed up with plates of food for everyone at the table except Slocum. After the plates had been distributed and the coffee cups refilled, the waiter left. Diglo looked across at Slocum.

"Cousin Slocum," he said, "you look as if Cousin Romp gave you a hell of a good drubbing. Sorry. But I heard all about the fight you had with him—shortly before he was murdered. Oh, don't get me wrong. I didn't mean anything by that. Not anything accusatory. I know that you were in your bath at the time he was killed. Besides, from all that I've heard, I wouldn't think that would be your style, to kill a man in his bath—that is, if you wanted to kill him in the first place."

"I'd thought about it," said Slocum. "Given a little more time, I might even have gotten around to it."

"Yes," said Diglo, "I dare say. Cousin Romp could test one's patience at times."

"Well, if there was any drubbing about it," Cofy said, "it went both ways, and that's for sure. It was a hell of a fight, it was, and a close one to call."

"Oh, yes," said Diglo. "I remember you said that before. I suppose that it's just because I'm looking at Cousin Slocum here, and I didn't get a chance to see Cousin Romp."

"You didn't, huh?" Slocum asked.

"No," said Diglo. "I didn't. I just arrived this morning."

"Oh, yeah. So you said. And they told you about the fight and about the killing last night," Slocum said. "They tell you about all the other killings? They tell you that the three of us here at the table are the only heirs left out of a whole mess of them that was here?"

"Yes," said Diglo. "They told me all that."

"Only just a few minutes ago?"

"Yes. Shortly after I arrived."

"You ain't real tore up about it, are you?" said Slocum. Diglo shrugged.

"The family," he said, "what was left of it, was not very close. You, of all of us, should understand that."

"I reckon," Slocum said.

Lewes finished his meal and drank the last of his coffee. He pushed his chair back away from the table.

"Well," he said, "until later then. I'll have a room reserved for us for the reading in the morning. If I don't see any of you before that, you can check at the desk to find out what room we'll be in."

Lewes got up to leave the room, and Diglo watched until he was out of earshot. Then, "A nervous little man, isn't he?" he said.

"Sarl," said Demmi, "if you'd been around the last few days with people getting murdered all around you, you'd be nervous, too."

Diglo laughed. "Yes," he said. "Yes, I dare say."

Demmi finished her meal and pushed herself back from the table. She glanced at Slocum.

"Let's go," he said.

Slocum shoved back his own chair and stood quickly, stepping behind her to pull hers out farther. "I'm ready," he said.

"Oh," said Diglo. "Could it be that something's going on between my two cousins here?"

"Whether there is or there ain't," said Slocum, "it's none of your damn business, and I suggest that you keep your mouth shut about it from here on."

Diglo laughed again. "My, my," he said. "I seem to have struck a nerve."

"Yeah?" said Slocum. "Well, see that you don't strike the same one again."

He started away from the table with Demmi, and Diglo turned toward Cofy. "Do you suppose he might murder me if I'm not careful?" he said.

"If he did I wouldn't blame him much," said Cofy, standing. "But I'm telling you to watch your mouth around here. There's already been enough trouble."

As Cofy left the room, Diglo chuckled to himself. Slocum and Demmi were still standing just inside the doorway when Cofy was about to go out. He paused and looked at them.

"I thought you two were leaving," he said.

There was an empty table there by the door, well across the room from where they had left Diglo sitting alone.

"I just decided I'm hungry after all," Slocum said. He pulled out a chair for Demmi and she sat. Then he pulled out another for himself.

"You're not thinking about starting anything up with that loud-mouthed surviving cousin of yours?" Cofy said.

"I'm only thinking about feeding my face," Slocum

said. He sat down and adjusted his seat a little so that he had a good view of Diglo where he sat.

"Well," said Cofy, "see that you don't start anything."

He walked on out the door, and Demmi turned to look hard at Slocum.

"John," she said, "what are you thinking of?"

"Did you see Diglo walk in here?" he asked her.

"Why, no," she said. "He was sitting there when I came in."

"I want to see if that son of a bitch walks with a limp on his left foot," Slocum said.

A waiter came to the table and Slocum ordered his breakfast. He watched Diglo and made small talk with Demmi. His breakfast arrived, and he ate. Diglo had not moved from his spot.

"John, are we going to sit here all day?" Demmi said.

"I mean to sit here long enough to see him get up and walk," said Slocum. "You don't need to stay."

"I'll stay for a while," she said. "I like your company."

"I'm afraid it ain't much good right now."

"It's better than anything else that's available," she said.

A waiter offered Diglo more coffee, and he accepted.

"He doesn't look as if he'll be getting up anytime soon," Demmi said.

"He'll have to pee sooner or later," said Slocum.

"Speaking of such things," said Demmi, "you'll have to excuse me for a few minutes."

Slocum stood to pull back her chair, and Demmi left the dining room. He sat back down. Diglo still sat at his table sipping his coffee. A waiter appeared at Slocum's table with a coffeepot.

"Sure," said Slocum, and the waiter refilled his cup. I guess I can last as long as that son of a bitch, Slocum told himself. But he was wrong. By the time Demmi returned, Slocum could just barely stand it.

"Keep your eye on him," he said, and he got up and left the room, walking at a quick pace. When he returned to the table a few minutes later, Demmi was still waiting for him, but Diglo was nowhere in sight. Slocum looked around, then quickly resumed his seat. He leaned over close to Demmi.

"Did you see him go?" he asked anxiously.

"Yes," she said. "Should I have followed him? I didn't know. I thought I should wait for you."

"Did he have a limp?"

"He walked out of here as straight as a board," Demmi said.

"You sure?" he asked, almost unbelieving. "He wasn't favoring one side even a little?"

"No," she said. "And he walked right by me. He smiled and tipped his hat as he passed me by."

"No limp," said Slocum.

"No limp."

"Damn," he said. "I knew it was him. Well, shit. Excuse me. I oughtn't to have said that, but I just knew that he'd have a limp. Hell, that puts me right back where I started."

"What do you mean?"

"If it ain't Diglo," said Slocum, "then who the hell is it?"

"What's so important about the limp?" she asked.

"Whoever it was that jumped me," Slocum said, "I stomped his left foot real good. I know I broke some bones."

20

Slocum didn't see anything more of Diglo all that day, and that night he again went to Demmi's room, not so much at her invitation as at her insistence. As he closed and latched the door behind himself, she stepped up close to him and put her head on his chest and her arms around him. She held him tight.

"John," she said, "I'm scared. Something's going to happen. The end is so close."

"Don't worry," he said.

"But something terrible's going to happen soon," she said. "I know it will."

"Well," he said, "I'm sticking right close to you, at least till this thing's all cleared up."

"At least until then," she said. "Oh, God, John, I don't know what I'd do if you weren't here."

She turned her face up, and he bent to kiss her lips, a soft, tender kiss. She had a taste and a smell so sweet that he almost forgot all the problems around them. Almost. He knew that she was afraid, and he knew that he had to comfort her and protect her. She was the one good thing that had happened to him during this whole crazy episode in his life, and he sure did want her to come out of it in good shape. Suddenly she broke loose from the embrace and took him by the hand, pulling him toward the bed.

"I need you close to me tonight," she said. "Real close."

"I'll stay close," he said.

Beside the bed, she started to undress. Slocum didn't need any more of an invitation than that. He could take a hint, so he started pulling off his own clothes. Soon the two of them were lying side by side, naked in bed.

Her hand reached over to fondle his crotch, first tickling and holding his balls, then inching up to grasp his cock, which was already growing in response to the more than welcome attention. She squeezed it hard, and it began to throb and jump in her grip.

"Oh," she said, "I think it's ready."

"You're damn right it's ready," he said.

"I want you behind me," she said. "Come at me from behind."

She rolled over and scrambled to her knees, grasping a bar of the wrought-iron bedstead in each hand. Slocum moved around behind her on his own knees and sought out her cunt with the head of his cock. He found it wet and anxious, and when he knew that he was in just the right spot, he thrust forward with his hips, driving his rod deep into her warm, wet, and waiting tunnel of love.

She gasped out loud and arched her back, shoving her round, bare ass back against him. Slocum grasped a smooth cheek in each hand and began rocking back and forth, ramming in and out, and she responded in perfect timing.

"Oh, oh, oh," she cried.

His flesh slapped against hers, making the round ass cheeks bounce, and her dangling tits shook delightfully with the action.

"Oh, screw me hard, John," she said. "Screw me. Screw me. Screw me. I love it. Screw me."

He drove harder and faster, and his fingers dug into the

flesh of her butt. He felt the pressure welling up in his heavy balls, and he knew that the surge would come soon. He pounded against her, in and out of her honey pot. His lower stomach, his cock and balls, his upper thighs, all were wet and sticky from the juices of her cunt.

"Oh, John," she said. "Spank me. Spank me hard."

"What?" he said.

"Spank me," she said.

"What for?"

"Just do it," she said. "Do it."

During this brief exchange, their rhythmic motions had not ceased. Slocum raised a hand and slapped one cheek of Demmi's ass. She gasped.

"Again," she said. "Harder."

He swatted her again, this time on the other cheek, then again and again. He spanked her pretty ass with each thrust of his throbbing cock.

"Oh, oh, oh, oh," she said. "I'm coming. I'm coming."

He felt her juices running freely, and he felt the pressure in his own loins swelling even more. At last he felt it burst and spurt a tremendous shot that must have flooded her insides. He stopped spanking her, but he kept driving in and out, and with each forward thrust, he shot another load.

"Oh, God," she said. "Oh, you're filling me up."

He slowed his strokes, and then he stopped altogether, with his cock shoved all the way inside. He moved his hands up to her slim waist and pulled her back against him. He was panting, and she was sighing. He looked down at her round ass cheeks, now glowing red from the spanking he had given her. Soon his cock softened, and he backed up a little, allowing it to slip free.

As she rolled over onto her back, he got up and walked to the table across the room. He poured some water into the bowl and dipped a towel into it. He wrung it out and carried it back over to the bed.

"Here," he said.

Demmi took the towel and began washing Slocum's cock, balls, and all the surrounding area. When she had done with him, she spread her own legs and began swiping at her own crotch with the wet towel.

"That was wonderful," she said.

"It sure was," Slocum agreed.

Demmi rolled over to rest her head on his chest, and one arm reached around him. He put an arm around her and held her gently.

"I'm so glad you're here," she said. "I'd be scared to death alone."

"Demmi," he said, "I don't believe that you're scared of anything."

"I'm not usually," she said.

"But you are now?"

"Yes. It's the not knowing. Not knowing who's to blame, and not knowing what's next."

"Yeah," he said. "I know what you mean. But like I said, I'm going to stick right with you. You can relax. No one's going to touch you. Not as long as I'm here."

"No one but you," she said.

"Yeah," he said. "That's what I meant."

Soon they drifted off to sleep, side by side, naked and content, and Slocum's dreams were all pleasant.

He woke up to the sound of a loud scream very near to his ear, and he sat up straight in bed. Instinctively he reached for his Colt, which was hanging on the back of a chair just beside the bed. As he turned to grasp the weapon, he saw a figure at the open window, one leg already inside. He did not recognize the figure. It was only a silhouette, but he knew that it was not Diglo, for it was not large enough to be that unpleasant person.

All of these thoughts flashed through Slocum's mind as he jerked the Colt free from its holster, thumbed back the hammer, pointed toward the window, and fired. The explosion filled the small room. Demmi clapped her hands over her ears, and the mysterious figure at the window yelped and vanished. Slocum jumped out of bed and ran to the window. He looked out, but no one was there.

"It's okay," he said. "He's gone."

"Who was it?"

"I don't know," he said. He had his left hand resting on the window ledge as he stood looking out, and then he realized that he was touching something wet and sticky.

"Demmi," he said. "Light the lamp."

She did, and he moved over into the light, holding his left hand out.

"What is it?" she said.

"Blood," he said. "I hit him."

He picked up the lamp and moved back to the window. Sure enough, there was blood on the windowsill. He leaned out with the lamp and noted more blood spilled on the landing just outside.

"I got him good," he said. "But we better get dressed. That shot likely woke up the whole damn hotel. If we had any secret from anyone, we won't anymore."

Just then there was a loud knock at the door, followed by the voice of Chief Cofy.

"Hello," Cofy said. "Hello in there. Miss Bloe. Are you all right? Open the door."

"Better answer him," Slocum said, pulling on his trousers.

Demmi grabbed a robe and wrapped it around herself as she answered Cofy's questions with a loud voice.

"I'm all right," she said. "Just a minute."

She moved across the room, unlatched the door, then opened it slightly. Peering out, she could see Lewes and Diglo and a few others in the hallway.

"Come in, Chief," she said. "Just you."

Cofy looked over his shoulder at the small crowd behind him.

"Run along now," he said. "Everything's under control here."

He slipped sideways through the small opening which Demmi allowed, and as soon as he was in the room, she shut the door and relatched it. Cofy looked at Slocum standing in the middle of the room, wearing nothing but his trousers, his Colt still in his hand. The room was filled with smoke and the acrid smell of burnt gunpowder. Cofy looked from Slocum to Demmi, and Demmi blushed slightly.

"We were just—"

"Never mind about that," Cofy said. "Just tell me what the hell happened in here."

Slocum nodded toward the window and held up the light, and Cofy stepped over for a look. He saw the blood.

"Son of a bitch was halfway in the room," Slocum said.

"Who?" said Cofy. "Who was it?"

"Couldn't tell," said Slocum. "But I sure as hell hit him."

"I'd say so," said the policeman, leaning out the window and looking at the blood on the landing. "We'll damn sure know him if we see him in the morning. I'd bet he even left us a trail to follow. A trail of blood."

"Yeah," said Slocum. "We'd have a hell of a time trying to follow it in the dark, though."

"I'll get on it with first light," Cofy said. "This may be the break we needed on this case. Good work, Slocum."

"Cofy," Slocum said. "I'm going with you in the morning."

The policeman straightened up and looked at Slocum for a moment. He stroked his chin.

"Sure," he said. "Sure. Why not?"

"One other thing," Slocum said.

"What's that?"

"Whoever that son of a bitch was, it wasn't Diglo."

"I thought you couldn't see him well enough to identify him," Cofy said.

"All I saw," said Slocum, "was an outline, but it wasn't a big enough outline for Diglo. I'm sure of that."

Cofy scratched his head and muttered. "Hmm," he said. He started for the door. "Oh, by the way. I'll tell everyone that Miss Bloe fired the shot. If you like."

"Thanks," said Slocum. "We appreciate that."

21

Slocum was up at the crack of dawn. He woke Demmi up and made her get dressed to go downstairs to the dining room.

"I'm going with Cofy," he said, "and I don't want you up here by yourself."

He met the policeman in the lobby and made sure that other police were on duty in the hotel. One was stationed just at the door to the dining room. Slocum also noticed that Diglo was back, already seated and drinking his morning coffee. He gave Diglo a hard look, and Diglo returned a smile. Slocum fought off an urge to throw some serious questions at the man, but he knew that he had more important things to deal with at the moment. He turned to Cofy.

"You ready?" he asked.

"Let's go," said Cofy.

They went outside and around the building to the spot where the fire escape came down from Demmi's room. They found some blood there on the ground. Looking around, they found another spot a few feet away.

"You got him good, all right," said Cofy.

They followed the blood trail around to the alley and down to the next block. There it crossed the street and continued down the next alley. About halfway down that block, it stopped at the back door to a building.

"What's this place?" Slocum asked.

"The Hulbert Hotel," Cofy said. "It's a dive. Come on."

Cofy opened the door, and they went inside. The blood trail led them down the hallway to some stairs. They followed it up to the third floor, then down another hallway to the door to a room. Cofy looked at Slocum as he drew out his service revolver. Slocum pulled out his Colt. Then Cofy rapped his knuckles on the door. There was no response. He rapped again.

"Open up," he called through the door. "It's the police."

Still there was no response. Cofy turned again to Slocum.

"Stay here and watch," he said. "I'm going for a key."

While Cofy was gone, Slocum tried the door. It was locked. He knocked and called out for whoever was in there to open the door, but he had no better results than had Cofy. He was about to lose his patience when Cofy reappeared. A nervous little bald man accompanied him.

"Right here," said Cofy. "Open it up."

The man unlocked the door and stepped back quickly.

"You can go now," said Cofy, and the man almost ran back to the stairs. Cofy gave Slocum a look, and Slocum nodded. Cofy opened the door and pushed it all the way into the room. He stepped inside, revolver ready. Then he stood still. He tucked the revolver away and stepped on in.

"It's all right," he said.

Slocum followed him into the room. The bloody trail led to the bed, and Blenstool was stretched out on the bed, lying on blood-soaked sheets.

"Blenstool," said Cofy.

"I'll be damned," said Slocum. "Is the little son of a bitch dead?"

Cofy knelt beside the bed and leaned close to the detective. He could hear the faint sound of raspy breathing.

"He's still alive," he said. "I'd better get a doctor up here fast."

He started to stand, but Blenstool stopped him.

"Wait," he said, his voice not much more than a whisper. "It's no use. I'm done for."

Cofy leaned over the dying man.

"Was that you at Miss Bloe's window last night?" he asked.

"Yes," said Blenstool, his voice barely audible. "Who shot me?"

"I did," said Slocum.

Blenstool turned his head a little and tried to focus his vision.

"Slocum?" he said.

"It's me," Slocum said.

Blenstool chuckled and then coughed.

"Take it easy," said Cofy.

The coughing subsided, and Blenstool took a deep breath.

"It's fitting," he said. "Slocum."

"What the hell were you doing at that window?" Cofy asked.

"I went to kill Miss Bloe," the detective said.

"You?" said Cofy. "Has it been you all along then?"

A weak smile formed on Blenstool's pallid lips.

"Of course," he said. "Who else?"

"But why?"

"For Diglo," said the detective. "He paid me. He paid me well. What other reason is there?"

Cofy started to ask another question, but he knew that it would do no good. Blenstool would never speak again. He was dead. Cofy got slowly to his feet.

"Dead," he said.

"And I actually fought with the little son of a bitch," Slocum said. "I mean side by side with him, against the damned Suts. And that stranger on the train. I even liked him. Damn. I'd never have suspected him if I hadn't seen him sneak into the kitchen at the hotel the other day. Even then I didn't really suspect him."

"Well," said Cofy, "you were right about one thing."

"What's that?" Slocum asked.

"It was Diglo. Come on."

They went out and shut the door. Downstairs Cofy told the nervous clerk to go back up and lock the door again.

"And don't even look inside the room," he said. "I'll be sending another policeman over here right away. When he gets here, you unlock the door again for him. You got that?"

"Yes, sir," the man said, his voice trembling.

Slocum and Cofy walked back to the hotel. They stopped at the front desk to find out what room Lewes had reserved for the reading of the will, and then they hurried on to the meeting. Everyone looked at them as they stepped into the room.

"Ah," said Lewes, "here he is. We can proceed now."

Diglo jerked a thumb toward Cofy.

"Does he have to be in here?" he asked. "I thought this was to be a private reading."

"Uh, in view of the circumstances," Lewes said, "I think the chief has every right to be here. Now, uh, unless anyone has any other objections, I think we can proceed."

"Not quite yet, Mr. Lewes," Cofy said, stepping forward into the room. He was still standing behind where Diglo and Demmi were seated, facing Lewes over their heads.

"Not yet?" said Lewes. "Why, what's the matter?"

"Mr. Lewes," Cofy said, "you can cross one more name off your list."

"Why, I don't understand," said Lewes. "There are only three surviving heirs, and they're all here in the room."

"One of those three has been responsible for the murders that were done here," Cofy said, "and in this state a man can't profit from a killing he's responsible for."

"Who?" said Lewes.

"What is this?" said Diglo. "Let's get on with the reading."

"Mr. Diglo," said Cofy, "I'm asking you to come along with me. Don't give me any trouble."

"What for?" said Diglo, turning around in his chair to face Cofy.

"I'm placing you under arrest for the murders of Pug Kolp, Sten Comlo, Spig—uh, all of them. Come along peacefully now."

Diglo stood up, then turned suddenly, a small pocket pistol in his hand. He fired and the slug ripped into Cofy's right shoulder. Cofy spun with the impact and the pain, and Slocum whipped out his Colt and sent a slug into Diglo's chest. Diglo stood swaying, looking down at the fresh hole in his chest and the spreading dark stain on his white shirt. His eyes opened wide in surprised disbelief. Then he pitched forward over the chair he had been sitting in.

O'Hara and another policeman appeared in the doorway with revolvers in their hands.

"What's going on here?" O'Hara demanded.

"Nothing," said Slocum. "It's all over. You'd better see to your boss there, though."

Cofy was taken out to be tended by a doctor, and the body of Diglo was removed. Even so, Lewes suggested they move to a new location for the reading of the will.

"Hell," said Slocum, "there's only just three of us here. Let's go to the bar and have a drink."

"Well," said Lewes, "it's highly irregular."

"Is there a rule against it?" Slocum asked.

"Well, no. I don't think so."

Demmi grabbed Slocum with one arm and Lewes with the other.

"Then let's go to the bar," she said.

They ordered a bottle of good bourbon and a carafe of white wine for Demmi. Then they found a relatively private table in a far corner of the room and sat down and poured their drinks.

"All right, Mr. Lewes," Slocum said, "let's hear it."

Lewes cleared his throat and broke the seal on the document he held. He started to read the opening legalistic language, but Slocum cut him short.

"We've put up with enough bullshit on this deal," he said. "Just get to the heart of it. What did the old son of a bitch leave us?"

"How much money?" Demmi asked.

"Well, uh, let's see here," said Lewes, scanning the paper quickly. "Uh, no money."

"None?" Demmi asked.

"Not a dime beyond the expense money which we've already used up here at the hotel."

Slocum threw back his head and roared with laughter. Demmi looked at him, slightly indignant, then smiled. At last she, too, started to laugh. Lewes waited patiently for their laughter to subside.

"There is some property," he said.

"What kind of property?" said Demmi.

"Where?" Slocum asked.

"It's a business in Creed, Colorado," Lewes said. "Apparently quite profitable."

"What kind of business?" Slocum asked.

Lewes blushed a deep red.

"Well," he said, "it's, uh, a bawdy house, a house of ill repute."

"You mean a whorehouse?" Slocum asked.

"Well, yes," said Lewes, "to put it bluntly. Yes. And the two of you are the sole owners."

Slocum looked at Demmi, then back at Lewes.

"Partners?" he said.

"Yes," said the lawyer. "Fifty-fifty."

"Hell," said Slocum "I ain't sure that's a fit business for a lady."

"Oh, pooh, John," said Demmi. "Mr. Lewes, did you say this—establishment—was profitable?"

"Yes, indeed."

"In that case," she said, looking back at Slocum, "I'd call it a fit business. When do we head west, Partner?"

Slocum scratched his head.

"I don't know," he said. "Oh, hell, I'm ready to head west, all right, but I can't see myself as a businessman. For sure not that business. I don't want it, Mr. Lewes. Strike my name off of there and give the place to Demmi."

"You're entitled to half, Mr. Slocum," said the lawyer. "If you're not interested, perhaps Miss Bloe could buy out your interest."

"I don't have that kind of money," Demmi said.

"You say it's mine?" Slocum asked.

"Half is yours," said Lewes.

"If it's mine, then I can give it away," said Slocum. "Give it all to Demmi."

Demmi turned to face Slocum. She put a hand on his arm and smiled into his eyes.

"If that's the way you want it, John," she said. "But you'll always be welcome. I'll always consider that it's half yours, and there will always be money in the bank for you."

"I'll, uh, I'll make the necessary changes," Lewes said.

"And I'll be riding west," said Slocum. "It's been fun."

He started for the door, but Demmi stopped him.

"John?" she said. "Just like that?"

"It's still early in the day," he said. "If I get going, I can put a few miles between me and this damn city."

"John," she said, "I don't want to go all the way to Creed by myself."

"I ain't getting on another damn train," he said.

"Couldn't we get a horse for me?" she asked.

"Can you ride?"

"Of course I can."

"It's going to be a long ride," he said.

"I don't mind."

"Well, by God," Slocum said. "Mr. Lewes, telegraph whatever you need to right out to the whorehouse. Tell them their new boss is on the way, but she won't be there in a hurry. So long."

He took Demmi by the arm and walked out the door of the bar.

"Let's go get our things out of the rooms, girl," he said. "Then we'll find you a horse, and we'll get to riding."

"Riding west," she said.

"Riding west," he repeated. "All the way to your new place of business."

"My whorehouse," she said, nearly shouting with joy. "My own pleasure palace. When we get there, do you think that you might hang around for a little while?"

Slocum stopped walking, put his hands on her shoulders, and turned her toward him. He looked down into her eyes. They were big and bright and beautiful. Her shoulders were bare, and he could even see the cleavage in front, which invited him to seek out further pleasures.

"Well, yes, ma'am," he said. "I just might be persuaded."

SPECIAL PREVIEW

They were the most brutal gang of cutthroats ever assembled. And during the Civil War, they sought justice outside of the law. Paying back every Yankee raid with one of their own. They rode hard, shot straight, and had their way with every willing woman west of the Mississippi. No man could stop them. No woman could resist them. And no Yankee stood a chance of living when Quantrill's Raiders rode into town . . .

BUSHWHACKERS
by B. J. Lanagan

Available in paperback from Jove Books

And now here's a special excerpt from
this thrilling new series . . .

Jackson County, Missouri, 1862

As Seth Coulter lay his pocket watch on the bedside table and blew out the lantern, he thought he saw a light outside. Walking over to the window, he pulled the curtain aside to stare out into the darkness.

On the bed alongside him the mattress creaked, and his wife, Irma, raised herself on her elbows.

"What is it, Seth?" Irma asked. "What are you lookin' at?"

"Nothin', I reckon."

"Well, you're lookin' at somethin'."

"Thought I seen a light out there, is all."

Seth continued to look through the window for a moment longer. He saw only the moon-silvered West Missouri hills.

"A light? What on earth could that be at this time of night?" Irma asked.

"Ah, don't worry about it," Seth replied, still looking through the window. "It's prob'ly just lightning bugs."

"Lightning bugs? Never heard of lightning bugs this early in the year."

"Well it's been a warm spring," Seth explained. Finally, he came away from the window, projecting to his wife an easiness he didn't feel. "I'm sure it's nothing," he said.

"I reckon you're right," the woman agreed. "Wisht the boys was here, though."

Seth climbed into bed. He thought of the shotgun over

175

the fireplace mantel in the living room, and he wondered if he should go get it. He considered it for a moment, then decided against it. It would only cause Irma to ask questions, and just because he was feeling uneasy, was no reason to cause her any worry. He turned to her and smiled.

"What do you want the boys here for?" he asked. "If the boys was here, we couldn't be doin' this." Gently, he began pulling at her nightgown.

"Seth, you old fool, what do you think you're doin'?" Irma scolded. But there was a lilt of laughter in her voice, and it was husky, evidence that far from being put off by him, she welcomed his advances.

Now, any uneasiness Seth may have felt fell away as he tugged at her nightgown. Finally she sighed.

"You better let me do it," she said. "Clumsy as you are, you'll like-as-not tear it."

Irma pulled the nightgown over her head, then dropped it onto the floor beside her bed. She was forty-six years old, but a lifetime of hard work had kept her body trim, and she was proud of the fact that she was as firm now as she had been when she was twenty. She lay back on the bed and smiled up at her husband, her skin glowing silver in the splash of moonlight. Seth ran his hand down her nakedness, and she trembled under his touch. He marvelled that, after so many years of marriage, she could still be so easily aroused.

Three hundred yards away from the house, Emil Slaughter, leader of a band of Jayhawkers, twisted around in his saddle to look back at the dozen or so riders with him. Their faces were fired orange in the flickering lights of the torches. Felt hats were pulled low, and they were all wearing long dusters, hanging open to provide access to the pistols which protruded from their belts. His band of followers looked,

Slaughter thought, as if a fissure in the earth had suddenly opened to allow a legion of demons to escape from hell. There was about them a hint of sulphur.

A hint of sulphur. Slaughter smiled at the thought. He liked that idea. Such an illusion would strike fear into the hearts of his victims, and the more frightened they were, the easier it would be for him to do his job.

Quickly, Slaughter began assigning tasks to his men.

"You two hit the smokehouse, take ever' bit of meat they got a'curin'."

"Hope they got a couple slabs of bacon," someone said.

"I'd like a ham or two," another put in.

"You three, go into the house. Clean out the pantry, flour, corn-meal, sugar, anything they got in there. And if you see anything valuable in the house, take it too."

"What about the people inside?"

"Kill 'em," Slaughter said succinctly.

"Women, too?"

"Kill 'em all."

"What about their livestock?"

"If they got any ridin' horses, we'll take 'em. The plowin' animals, we'll let burn when we torch the barn. All right, let's go."

In the bedroom Seth and Irma were oblivious to what was going on outside. Seth was over her, driving himself into her moist triangle. Irma's breathing was coming faster and more shallow as Seth gripped her buttocks with his hands, pulling her up to meet him. He could feel her fingers digging into his shoulders, and see her jiggling, sweat-pearled breasts as her head flopped from side to side with the pleasure she was feeling.

Suddenly Seth was aware of a wavering, golden glow on

the walls of the bedroom. A bright light was coming through the window.

"What the hell?" he asked, interrupting the rhythm and holding himself up from her on stiffened arms, one hand on each side of her head.

"No, no," Irma said through clenched teeth. "Don't stop now, don't . . ."

"Irma, my God! The barn's on fire!" Seth shouted, as he disengaged himself.

"What?" Irma asked, now also aware of the orange glow in the room.

Seth got out of bed and started quickly, to pull on his trousers. Suddenly there was a crashing sound from the front of the house as the door was smashed open.

"Seth!" Irma screamed.

Drawing up his trousers, Seth started toward the living room and the shotgun he had over the fireplace.

"You lookin' for this, you Missouri bastard?" someone asked. He was holding Seth's shotgun.

"Who the hell are . . ." That was as far as Seth got. His question was cut off by the roar of the shotgun as a charge of double-aught buckshot slammed him back against the wall. He slid down to the floor, staining the wall behind him with blood and guts from the gaping exit wounds in his back.

"Seth! My God, no!" Irma shouted, running into the living room when she heard the shotgun blast. So concerned was she about her husband that she didn't bother to put on her nightgown.

"Well, now, lookie what we got here," a beady-eyed Jayhawker said, staring at Irma's nakedness. "Boys, I'm goin' to have me some fun."

"No," Irma said, shaking now, not only in fear for her

own life, but in shock from seeing her husband's lifeless body leaning against the wall.

Beady Eyes reached for Irma.

"Please," Irma whimpered. She twisted away from him. "Please."

"Listen to her beggin' me for it, boys. Lookit them titties! Damn, she's not a bad-lookin' woman, you know that?" His dark beady eyes glistened, rat-like, as he opened his pants then reached down to grab himself. His erection projected forward like a club.

"No, please, don't do this," Irma pleaded.

"You wait 'til I stick this cock in you, honey," Beady Eyes said. "Hell, you goin' to like it so much you'll think you ain't never been screwed before."

Irma turned and ran into the bedroom. The others followed her, laughing, until she was forced against the bed.

"Lookit this, boys! She's brought me right to her bed! You think this bitch ain't a'wantin' it?"

"I beg of you, if you've any kindness in you . . ." Irma started, but her plea was interrupted when Beady Eyes backhanded her so savagely that she fell across the bed, her mouth filled with blood.

"Shut up!" he said, harshly. "I don't like my women talkin' while I'm diddlin' 'em!"

Beady Eyes came down onto the bed on top of her, then he spread her legs and forced himself roughly into her. Irma felt as if she were taking a hot poker inside her, and she cried out in pain.

"Listen to her squealin'. He's really givin' it to her," one of the observers said.

Beady Eyes wheezed and gasped as he thrust into her roughly.

"Don't wear it out none," one of the others giggled. "We'uns want our turn!"

At the beginning of his orgasm, Beady Eyes enhanced his pleasure by one extra move that was unobserved by the others. Immediately thereafter he felt the convulsive tremors of the woman beneath him, and that was all it took to trigger his final release. He surrendered himself to the sensation of fluid and energy rushing out of his body, while he groaned and twitched in orgiastic gratification.

"Look at that! He's comin' in the bitch right now!" one of the others said excitedly. "Damn! You wait 'til I get in there! I'm goin' to come in quarts!"

Beady Eyes lay still on top of her until he had spent his final twitch, then he got up. She was bleeding from a stab wound just below her left breast.

"My turn," one of the others said, already taking out his cock. He had just started toward her when he saw the wound in the woman's chest, and the flat look of her dead eyes. "What the hell?" he asked. "What happened to her?"

The second man looked over at Beady Eyes in confusion. Then he saw Beady Eyes wiping blood off the blade of his knife.

"You son of bitch!" he screamed in anger. "You kilt her!"

"Slaughter told us to kill her," Beady Eyes replied easily.

"Well, you coulda waited 'til someone else got a chance to do her before you did it, you bastard!" The second man putting himself back into his pants, started toward Beady Eyes when, suddenly, there was the thunder of a loud pistol shot.

"What the hell is going on in here?" Slaughter yelled. He was standing just inside the bedroom door, holding a smoking pistol in his hand, glaring angrily at them.

"This son of a bitch kilt the woman while he was doin' her!"

"We didn't come here to screw," Slaughter growled. "We come here to get supplies."

"But he kilt her *while* he was screwin' her! Who would do somethin' like that?"

"Before, during, after, what difference does it make?" Slaughter asked. "As long as she's dead. Now, you've got work to do, so get out there in the pantry, like I told you, and start gatherin' up what you can. You," he said to Beady Eyes, "go through the house, take anything you think we can sell. I want to be out of here in no more'n five minutes."

"Emil, what woulda been the harm in us havin' our turn?"

Slaughter cocked the pistol and pointed it at the one who was still complaining. "The harm is, I told you not to," he said. "Now, do you want to debate the issue?"

"No, no!" the man said quickly, holding his hands out toward Slaughter. "Didn't mean nothin' by it. I was just talkin', that's all."

"Good," Slaughter said. He looked over at Beady Eyes. "And you. If you ever pull your cock out again without me sayin' it's all right, I'll cut the goddamned thing off."

"It wasn't like you think, Emil," Beady Eyes said. "I was just tryin' to be easy on the woman, is all. I figured it would be better if she didn't know it was about to happen."

Slaughter shook his head. "You're one strange son of a bitch, you know that?" He stared at the three men for a minute, then he shook his head in disgust as he put his pistol back into his belt. "Get to work."

Beady Eyes was the last one out and as he started to leave he saw, lying on the chifferobe, a gold pocket watch. He glanced around to make sure no one was looking.

Quickly, and unobserved, he slipped the gold watch into his own pocket.

This was a direct violation of Slaughter's standing orders. Anything of value found on any of their raids was to be divided equally among the whole. That meant that, by rights, he should give the watch to Slaughter, who would then sell it and divide whatever money it brought. But because it was loot, they would be limited as to where they could sell the watch. That meant it would bring much less than it was worth and by the time it was split up into twelve parts, each individual part would be minuscule. Better, by far, that he keep the watch for himself.

Feeling the weight of the watch riding comfortably in his pocket, he went into the pantry to start clearing it out.

"Lookie here!" the other man detailed for the pantry said. "This here family ate pretty damn good, I'll tell you. We've made us quite a haul: flour, coffee, sugar, onions, potatoes, beans, peas, dried peppers."

"Yeah, if they's as lucky in the smokehouse, we're goin' to feast tonight!"

The one gathering the loot came into the pantry then, holding a bulging sack. "I found some nice gold candlesticks here, too," he said. "We ought to get somethin' for them."

"You men inside! Let's go!" Slaughter's shout came to them.

The Jayhawkers in the house ran outside where Slaughter had brought everyone together. Here, they were illuminated by the flames of the already-burning barn. Two among the bunch were holding flaming torches, and they looked at Slaughter expectantly.

With a nod of his head, Slaughter said, "All right, burn the rest of the buildings now."

JAKE LOGAN

TODAY'S HOTTEST ACTION WESTERN!

A special offer for people who enjoy reading the best Westerns published today.

WESTERNS!

NO OBLIGATION

Mail the coupon below

To start your subscription and receive 2 FREE WESTERNS, fill out the coupon below and mail it today. We'll send your first shipment which includes 2 FREE BOOKS as soon as we receive it.